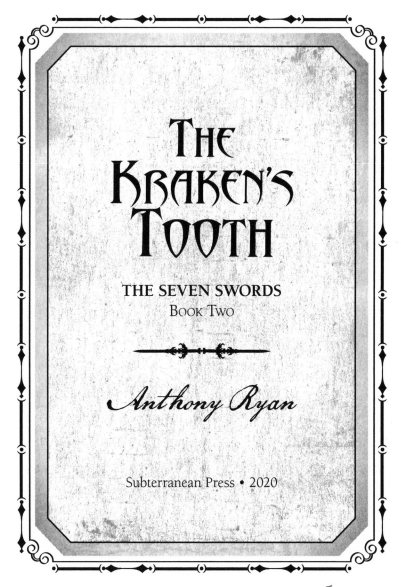

THE KRAKEN'S TOOTH

THE SEVEN SWORDS
BOOK TWO

Anthony Ryan

Subterranean Press • 2020

Edited by Yanni Kuznia

First Edition

ISBN
978-1-59606-979-4

Subterranean Press
PO Box 190106
Burton, MI 48519

subterraneanpress.com

Manufactured in the United States of America

Dedicated to the memory of the esteemed Dr. Henry Walton Jones, Professor of Archaeology at Barnett College NY and Marshall College Conn., whose landmark excavations in South America, Egypt and India provided a wellspring of inspiration for this story.

The chain that binds the body
is as nothing
to the chain that binds the soul.
—*Injunctions of the First Risen.*

Chapter One

JUSERIA'S GATE

•)———(•)———(•

"**N**o woman ever looked like that."

The monochrome paint covering Seeker's face creased as she squinted at the giant effigy rising above the distant bridge. Although it was much changed from Guyime's first glimpse of it so long ago, the statue's form retained a finely crafted, if somewhat improbably proportioned, clarity.

"Juseria was said to be the foremost beauty of her age," Guyime replied, turning the spitted goat haunch as the grease leaking from recently skinned flesh hissed into the fire.

Game was scarce in the scrub desert south of Sallish but there were times when travelling in company with a beast charmer had definite advantages. When Seeker had first returned from a lengthy nighttime disappearance with the cat in tow, Guyime had been skeptical of the beast's value. It was in many ways a stark contrast to the Chena, the massive hyena that had followed the woman throughout their unwise sojourn into the Execration. Whereas Chena had been all bulging shoulder muscle and bone-crushing jaws, Seeker's new companion was a red-pelted caracal usually found in more verdant country. It was roughly the same dimensions as a hunting hound with large, tufted ears, a body that was all spine, ribs and corded muscle and a tail as long as a slaver's whip. Seeker named her Lissah, her special insight revealing the beast had been driven away from her pack after attracting the attentions of the dominant male. "Cats," she said, "are as prone to jealousy as we are."

Guyime suspected that Lissah's solitary state had more to do with her foul temper. She met his every glance with bared fangs and a hiss, lashing out at any unwise expression of affection, as the row of scars on the back of his hand could testify. However, it was thanks to this tufted-eared, hissing horror that the hunger that had assailed them for the latter part of their trek from the Execration was no longer a problem. A cat's nose and ears would always find tracks missed by human eyes and the goat she had led Seeker to had provided sufficient sustenance to see them to their destination with meat to spare.

"Beauty or not," Seeker said, moving to squat opposite him, "tits so big and a waist so thin would make her little use in battle. I thought she was supposed to be a great warrior."

"That she was." Guyime raised his gaze to the statue, eyeing the dull greyish granite that formed the towering figure. "So great was her glory in life that her monument was burnished in gold. When it caught the fading sun on a clear day it was like the tallest beacon fire you ever saw."

"What happened to it?" Seeker took a knife and sliced off a small morsel of part-roasted meat, tossing it high into the air for Lissah. The cat could jump twice the height of a man from a sitting position and Seeker never tired of seeing her do it. "The gold."

"Stolen, claimed by the citizens or Sallish or stripped away by the elements." Guyime shrugged. "Her cult was already fading when I first came to the parts. In those days there were a few hundred worshippers encamped around the gate to the bridge, promising death to anyone who dared defile the monument to their beloved Divine Archer. If the gold's all gone, so are they."

"Gods die." Seeker's voice held a note of sour amusement but also hard conviction. "And their promises are always empty."

He heard the unspoken question beneath her words. As the only two survivors of the last ever pilgrimage to the heart of the Execration they had every reason to consider themselves recipients of near-miraculous good fortune, but their mood in the days since had been far from triumphant. Neither of their prayers had been answered; he was still a fallen king of dire reputation fated to bear the weight of a demon-cursed blade. She was still the bereft mother of a lost daughter she had risked everything to find. More than that, he knew that beneath the knowledge of failure lay the shadows inevitably left in the minds of those who had seen true demonic power with their own eyes. Such shadows could not be easily dispelled by the glimmer of hope they had found at the conclusion to their otherwise fruitless journey. *The seven cursed blades were set upon the earth for a purpose. To release the demons that dwell within them, that purpose must be fulfilled...*

"The Mad God wasn't truly a god," Guyime pointed out. "Just a demon summoned to the earthly realm by those arrogant enough to think they could control him. And I'm not sure death accurately describes his fate."

"Meaning he'll be suffering away in the Infernus, no doubt plotting revenge should he ever get free again."

The sword on Guyime's back gave off an abrupt, discomfiting thrum as the demon trapped within it stirred. Lakorath had slipped into a quiescent torpor in recent days as their journey wore on. It was his habit to adopt a state of vaguely aware dormancy during periods of tedium, but mention of the Infernus, and the creature they had banished there not long ago, would invariably stir his ire.

Tell the beast-loving bitch to shut her careless mouth, my liege, Lakorath instructed, the sword throbbing with each sharply uttered syllable. *A denizen of the first rank will sense mention of it in the mortal plane, even if you don't speak its name. We would do very well not to remind that one of our existence.*

"Do you really think he's ever likely to forget?" Guyime muttered back in irritation, provoking an angry shudder from the sword before Lakorath returned to sulky silence.

"What did it say?" Seeker enquired, the black and white paint forming a suspicious mask, narrowed eyes focusing on the sword handle jutting above Guyime's shoulder. Although she only ever heard Lakorath's words second hand, over the course of a trying journey they had been more than sufficient to engender a palpable, and mutual, dislike.

"Nothing of any import." Guyime tested the meat with his hunting knife and, seeing the juices run clear, cut himself a goodly portion. "As usual."

*S*leep eluded him come nightfall, as he knew it would. He told Seeker to forgo her share of the watch and spent the hours regarding the dwindling flames of the campfire before prowling the slopes of the hill in search of possible threats. The rise was tall enough to afford a clear view of the surrounding scrub and with the moon so high and bright it would be a foolish bandit indeed who chose to try their luck. Guyime found himself resenting the silver-speckled desert and its absence of danger. A distraction would have been welcome this night.

Restless, my liege? Lakorath asked, roused from his huff by the chance to land a jibe or two. *Why would that be, I wonder? Is this place, perhaps, a little too familiar?*

"Shut up," Guyime grunted, his boot sending a loose rock tumbling down the slope.

It wasn't always so empty a landscape, as I recall, Lakorath went on blithely. *Time was the lonely fire of two unescorted travellers would have attracted all manner of miscreants. But those were days of war and famine, not to mention a plague or two.* The sword gave off a faint vibration that told of a wistful sigh. *What a trial it is to live in peaceful times. Particularly so for you, I imagine. When you came here to claim me all those years ago I assume this place provided more than a few pleasing diversions, and those dozen loyal killers who used to traipse in your shadow.*

"Thirteen," Guyime corrected in a dull whisper, watching the dust stirred by the stone he had kicked.

Thirteen? But, I only recall twelve. Not that I could name any. It's the fate of mere followers to be forgotten, I find. You remember the actor playing the lead but not the faceless soldier standing at the back clutching a spear desperately trying to remember his one line. Do you remember them, I wonder?

"Yes." The rising dust seemed to linger in the air with unnatural sluggishness, taking on a discernable substance he ascribed to a trick played on the eyes by the over-bright moon, or his sleep-deprived mind. He could see them, vague figures formed in the lethargic dust. All of them, armed and armoured, faces hardened and scarred by war, and a boy, still not full-grown, a boy who followed King Guyime faithfully throughout his first exile. A boy who had followed him all the way to Sallish and never left. A boy named Ellipe.

"What a wondrous thing!" he had exclaimed upon catching sight of Juseria's gleaming monument. Ellipe tried to maintain a manly demeanour at most times, deepening his voice and moulding his unmarked, beardless features into an unconvincing parody of the scowl habitually worn by his fellows. But that day, when confronted with one of the most renowned wonders in all the Five Seas, he became a boy again.

"I hadn't imagined there was enough gold in all the world," he went on, eyes reflecting the gleam of the sun on the metal. His voice was high and the vowels well spoken, the legacy of his education, an uncommon trait amongst the close companions of King Guyime who preferred to raise up deserving souls rather than favour those born to privilege.

"Fucking waste, y'ask me," Leonne had said, the grey whiskered crags of his face bunching in righteous disapproval. "How many beggars did we pass on the road? A lot of empty bellies could be fed with that thing."

Leonne, like most of the souls that comprised this company of dispossessed knights and men-at-arms, was a man of many contradictions. Guyime had seen him slit the throats of a dozen useless captives in the aftermath of battle then rifle their corpses for valuables. A good portion of the loot would be spent at the grog waggon but most he would hand out to the hordes of displaced villages that invariably clustered on the fringes of the

Ravager's army. When Guyime had knighted him he took the title 'Sir Leonne of the Kindly Hand,' however throughout the long years of their association, his hand remained as deft and ruthless with a knife as it was generous with alms.

I remember that one, Lakorath said as Guyime's gaze tracked over the parade of dusty ghosts. *Took a dozen arrows to kill him at Saint Maree's Field. The tall one lost half his skull to a mace. The woman with the crossbow died screaming with her hands buried in her sundered guts...*

"Enough!" Guyime grated, which, of course, only encouraged the demon to intensify his taunts.

Don't recall the boy, though. The wind shifted, causing the dust-crafted ghosts to slip away, all save one. Ellipe, still standing rapt by the sight of the golden statue, probably the most beautiful thing his eyes ever witnessed in all too short a life. *Meaning he must have perished in Sallish,* Lakorath concluded. *Care to elaborate as to how and why, my liege?*

It was rare these days for fury to claim Guyime, the times when it could strip away his reason and lead to all manner of unfortunate complications were mostly in the past, but not completely. A grunt of bestial anger emerged from between his clenched teeth as he drew the sword, whirling to cast it away, send it spinning into the desert where it could lie for centuries for all he cared. Let it be covered by the sand, a discarded forgotten prison for so pestilent a soul...

The sword handle slipped barely an inch along his callused palm before abruptly becoming as weighty as an anvil. Sand blossomed as the blade sliced into the ground, dragging Guyime down with it, so heavy it pinned his hand beneath the handle, pain joining with fury as he tried vainly to tug it free.

Really? Lakorath asked with arch disdain. *After all this time, you still haven't learned this particular lesson?*

The blade began to glow, smoke rising and sand hissing as the heat turned it to glass.

We are bound, my liege. Lakorath's voice possessed no humour now, just implacable certainty, and also a measure of regret. After all, he was as much Guyime's slave as his tormentor. *You to me and me to you. You cannot discard me. You cannot sell me. You cannot destroy me.*

"Wrong!" Guyime hissed back, sweat beading his face as the heat grew and the sword pressed his hand deeper into the sand, skin prickling as muscle and bone strained under the pressure. "The Seven Swords. When I have them…"

Lakorath laughed. Demon laughter, an ugly, grating ripple of amusement. *So, that's your true plan,* he said. *So much for your lofty ambitions of uniting the seven demon-cursed blades in order to rid the world of the Risen Church. You think that by bringing them together you'll somehow fulfil the purpose for which they were created, whatever that might be. Then you will finally be free. Is that it, my liege?*

The sword's glow faded and its weight returned to normal, allowing Guyime to heft it once more. The handle thrummed with amused satisfaction as he slid the blade into the scabbard on his back. "Yes!" he snarled, seeing little reason to conceal his design, or his hatred for the creature he was forced to carry. "If I fulfil the destiny of the seven swords, there will no longer be a reason for your existence, demon."

And what do you think it might be? This fabled destiny?

"You mean you don't know?"

I know only that I was trapped in this blade a very long time ago. I have been wielded by heroes of legend and villains of infamy. By the worst scum and the most noble spirit. And in all that time you know what I learned, my liege? There was no meaning in any of it, no purpose that counted for more than shit in the end. Heroes win their wars only to become tyrants. The worst of murderers may escape punishment but cannot escape their own souls and they will always die pitiful, friendless and unmourned. The Infernus is an eternal plane of chaos and agony, but this world is worse. Vile we may be but at least a demon knows what it is. Mortals live their entire existence flailing in the effluent of their own delusions. By all means find the swords, set me free or destroy me. But don't look for purpose when it's done as I suspect all you'll find is death.

Chapter Two

THE CARTOGRAPHER

As they passed beneath Juseria's statue the following morning, Guyime saw that she wasn't completely denuded of gold after all. As the rising sun played over her neck and face he caught flickers of light amongst the grey stone that told of stubborn treasure still clinging to her impossibly magnificent features.

"Too high to climb for most," a camel drover explained. He was a tall, swarthy fellow with a tulwar on his back and bright, cheerful eyes peering out from the silks covering his head. Guyime recalled that it was custom for men born to the region to conceal their faces from Juseria's gaze as they traversed the bridge she guarded. Apparently it stemmed from an ancient superstition that she would come to life at the sight of a man who reminded her of the lover she had lost in the Kraken Wars. As he and Seeker trekked towards the bridge Guyime had fixed a scarf around his own face so as not to arouse any local animosity.

"A few dozen still try it every year," the drover went on. "And end up falling to their deaths as a reward. Most beggar-folk are more patient and just wait for it to fall off." He gestured to a cluster of people in ragged, unkempt garb hovering around each of Juseria's massive feet, every face lit with tense, hopeful expectation. "Best not to be here when it happens, though," the drover added. "The place becomes a battlefield. The last poor sod who caught a falling nugget got chased into the river for it. Curious thing though, when the city guards dragged his corpse from the shallows, he still had hold of the gold."

"There were no beggars here when last I came to Sallish," Guyime commented. "The Archer's Cult decreed anyone begging for alms within Divine Juseria's sight should be beheaded on the spot."

"Then you must be older than you look, friend. The last dregs of the cult got wiped out near thirty years ago, may the Infernus claim their souls. These days, the only objects of worship in Sallish are money and profit."

Entry to the city required payment of one silver coin apiece to the guardsmen plus a copper for Lissah. The sight of an unfettered caracal walking with a large grizzled man of brutish aspect and a woman with a paint-covered face aroused some lingering glances from the people thronging the streets beyond the bridge, but no unwelcome attention. As one of the principal ports on the southern shore of the Second Sea, the people of Sallish were well accustomed to all manner of visitors. They passed a number of folk in outlandish garb beyond even Guyime's experience, few of whom stirred any particular interest amongst the bustling populace.

Even though Seeker's search for her daughter had brought her here before, her face betrayed the wrinkle-nosed dislike of one born to the wilds when confronted with the smell and noise of a city. The air was rich in mingled spices and the scent of roasting meats, a pall of steam and smoke rising from the carts of the vendors to linger over each packed thoroughfare. Guyime found the purposeful chaos of the place little changed from his previous visit, although he fancied his ear detected a few more unfamiliar dialects amongst the general din. Amidst the overlapping babble there was, of course, another sound he remembered all too well.

The whip's crack was loud enough to pain the ears, the scream that followed it more painful to the soul in its utter despair and agony. Grumbles and curses swallowed the fading scream as the crowd shuffled to the fringes of the street, the variously hued faces regarding the passing line of chained, naked people with more irritation than pity. The slaves numbered a dozen, all manacled at the wrists and linked collar to collar by a chain. They were led by a brawny overseer, blood dripping from the three-tongued tip of his ox-hide lash as he tugged his merchandise towards the docks, a trio of guards following with their own whips at the ready to quicken the step of any unfortunate laggards.

Guyime watched the disdain on Seeker's face transform into something less expressive but far more threatening. Her eyes were bright and keen as they slipped from the face of one slave to another. They were all men but for the young woman at the rear, stumbling along with her head lowered and grease-matted hair veiling her face. Guyime knew from the slave's colouring and age she couldn't be the object of Seeker's interest, but still the beast charmer took an involuntary step forward, Lissah letting out an anticipatory hiss as she sensed the woman's intent.

"We have other business," Guyime said, lightly touching Seeker's shoulder. He knew better than to take a firmer hold. They shared a purpose, for now, but this woman was not within his command nor was she the kind to forgive a grabbing hand.

She stiffened but stayed in place, turning her gaze from the female slave as she passed by, sobbing with every step. Watching Seeker conceal the anguish that threatened to disorder her features, Guyime knew she was imagining many such horrors that had almost certainly been visited upon an even younger victim.

"I told you we'll find her," he said. "For all the bad I've done, I've not yet broken a promise."

Her eyes flashed at him in unexpected anger, no doubt born of the ugliness they had just witnessed. "When I tracked down the captain of the slavers who stole my daughter," she said, "he made me many promises too, and died for the lies he told. It was not a quick death, Pilgrim."

Guyime raised an eyebrow. She had learned his true name weeks ago but continued to address him by the title he had chosen at the commencement of their journey into the Execration, although he noticed she tended to employ it in moments of anger or suspicion. Also, she made no effort to acquaint him with her name, insisting he continue to call her only Seeker. "You think me a liar?" he asked.

"I think you are..." She trailed off with a sigh, the tension of imminent combat leaching away. "Complicated." She nodded at the sword on his back. "Has that *thing* offered any insight as yet?"

"No, nor would I expect him to." Guyime turned, casting around until he saw a familiar alley leading to a quarter known to the locals as the Misted Lanes. "We came here for insight of a different sort."

The only aspect of the Cartographer's shop that had changed was the Cartographer herself. When Guyime had last stepped through this door he had been confronted by a woman who would have been tall but for her stooped back, a face of once-aquiline beauty wrinkled and spotted with age. She had moved painfully around the cramped confines of her shop, gnarled hands clutching the stick she used to spare her knees. Now, instead of an old woman, they were greeted by what a less keen eye might have taken for her granddaughter. She stood tall and straight, clad in plain silks of grey and black, the face smooth and pleasing with its high cheekbones and softly curving chin. However, one glance at her eyes left Guyime in no doubt as to who he looked upon.

"You're younger," he said, stepping inside. Seeker followed after a moment's suspicious hesitation whilst Lissah lingered in the doorway, baring her fangs. Guyime couldn't fault the caracal's instincts; there was a great deal of danger in this place.

"And you're older," the Cartographer returned, angling her head as she studied him. "Though not as old as you should be." Her gaze snapped to the open door where Seeker was making a vain attempt to encourage Lissah to enter. "Take your beast outside or leave it in the street," the Cartographer snapped, her voice very much that of the old woman she had once been. "I don't like draughts."

Seeker's face tensed at the woman's rudeness but she quickly swallowed her anger. Crouching, she held Lissah's gaze for a second, the cat staring back in immobile fascination before blinking and bounding away to ascend the wall opposite the shop, scaling it in a blurring frenzy of red fur and thrashing tail.

"Beast charmer, eh?" the Cartographer observed as Seeker closed the door. The Cartographer regarded Guyime with a frown of deepening curiosity. "Interesting company for a king."

"King no longer," he replied. "As I assume you know full well."

"I do occasionally take note of news from foreign climes, though not as much as I once did. It all becomes much the same after a few decades. Wars fought and lost, kingdoms risen and fallen. All rather dull for the most part, although I did hear of a recent event that was pleasingly out of the ordinary. It seems the Execration is no longer, well, the Execration."

"Yes." Guyime surveyed the shelves that lined the walls, each one laden with scrolled maps. As before there was no dust on any of them; the Cartographer kept her treasures well cared for. "I heard."

"All manner of rumours abound as to the cause," she went on. "Mostly nonsense about demon hordes boiling from the earth or somesuch. However, the more credible stories talk of a final pilgrimage, one that resulted in the Mad God's demise, a pilgrimage led by a northerner with a demon-cursed blade. In my very long life, I have encountered only one man who fits that description."

She stared into Guyime's eyes with a predatory hunger that others might have mistaken for carnal interest. He knew better. This woman had learned long ago that the only true wealth was knowledge, which at this juncture, made him both rich and in a position to bargain.

"Is it true?" she demanded in a low, guttural voice, stepping closer. "Did you kill him?"

Lakorath stirred at the Cartographer's approach, just a small cautionary tremble to the blade but she clearly sensed it, coming to an abrupt halt. "Are you here to do me harm, fallen king?" she enquired of Guyime, her bearing betraying a judicious caution but no excessive concern.

"I came for a map," he told her. "Draw it for me and I'll tell you all you want to know about the Execration and the Mad God."

"Maps are cursed amongst my people," Seeker told him in a faint, muttered hiss. They watched the Cartographer at work in the deep recesses of her shop, a gloomy space lit by a single lantern suspended over the tilted table where she laboured. She had locked the door before leading them here, making no further attempt to bargain a higher price. Perching herself at the table she unfurled a broad sheet of parchment, pinning the corners down before taking up a quill, dipping it in the ink well and starting to draw. She worked with a wordless intensity, completely absorbed in the lines she left on the parchment, lines which seemed mostly a chaotic mishmash of curves and angles. Guyime, however, had no doubt that chaos would resolve into clarity when she was done.

"Lines drawn across plains and mountains," Seeker went on, a note of disapproval creeping into her voice. "Drawn by those who don't even live there. Lines that become barriers to the passage of free folk who have walked the same paths for generations. Maps are the cages of kings and princes."

"It's not that kind of map," Guyime said. "She sees paths others don't, roads that lead to objects of desire, goals to be achieved, destinies to be fulfilled." *Roads often best left untravelled,* he added inwardly. He had asked the Cartographer two distinct questions, one for him and one for Seeker. Despite an instinctive certainty that every map this woman had ever drawn contained a trap for the one who had spent so much to purchase it, they would both follow their course regardless of where they might lead. Where else had they to go?

"She drew one for you before," Seeker said. "Where did it lead?"

"To him." Guyime inclined his head to the sword on his back. "Eventually to the Execration, now back here. It transpires the map she drew for me was a circle."

The Cartographer's quill didn't cease for several hours, nor did she once rise from the table. Watching her, Guyime saw an echo of her formerly aged self in the arch of her back and the concentrated focus on her face. He spent some time pondering the various unnatural means she may have employed to recover her youth until Lakorath drawled an obvious answer. *She drew herself a map, my liege. A chart describing the route to some magical wellspring of youth. Imagine the price such a thing could fetch. Many a king would gift you their entire domain for the chance at immortality. It must be around here somewhere...*

Guyime's gaze snapped to the Cartographer at the scrape of her chair on the floor tiles. She groaned as she rose and stepped back from the table, gesturing for him and Seeker to come closer. As expected, his first sight of the map revealed only a discordant melange of overlapping lines. Meaning would only be revealed when his price was paid.

"The Execration and the Mad God," the Cartographer said, voice tight with insistence. "Every part of it if you please."

So he told her, recounting each step of the journey, describing the fellow pilgrims lost along the way and the many horrors to be found in the Execration. He told her of the two doomed lovers, the youthful priest's murder at the hands of a treacherous fanatic, of the true demonic nature of the Mad God and the demon who had come to return him to the Infernus, saving Guyime and Seeker in the process. The Cartographer listened in silence to it all, face impassive though her eyes flicked continually between Guyime and Seeker, as if searching for some indication of a lie. If so, she found none and when he finished she gave a soft grunt of satisfaction.

"So the Execration lies empty," she mused. "One wonders what treasures the Mad God may have left in his wake."

"There's no treasure there," Seeker stated. "Just death."

"Perhaps, but I'm sure one day some greedy soul will turn up at my door with a yen to find out for sure. Knowing part of the answer before I hear the question always adds a clarity to the finished chart."

She gestured to the parchment on the table, the various lines broadening or extending to form a series of interlinked images. Curves morphed into mountains and angles into waves whilst one meaningless scrawl became a face, a face that brought a gasp to Seeker's lips.

"Ekiri!" She moved to the map, tremulous fingers hovering over the parchment as the face came fully into being. It was the face of a girl, perhaps twelve years old. Despite the monochrome paint that did much to conceal the true shape of Seeker's features, Guyime still discerned enough of a resemblance to the beast charmer to recognise her daughter. The girl's face lay at the centre of a complex web of lines, all but one tracing away to the edges of the map. Guyime followed this line to where it intersected with a pictogram he recognised as a miniature rendering of Sallish.

"Is she here?" he asked the Cartographer, receiving a shake of the head in response.

"Look closer."

Another line formed, tracing away from Sallish into the midst of the Second Sea where it abruptly veered west, coming to a halt when it met a second pictogram, a city, but the dimensions and form of it were odd, as if it were comprised of several huge slabs rising from the waves.

"Where is that?" Seeker demanded. The map held no script of any kind but Guyime knew the city's name, even though he had never been there.

"Carthula," he said, turning back to the Cartographer. "We'll find her there?"

"You find what you need to find there."

The woman's bland tone stirred his anger, much to Lakorath's satisfaction. *Such an obfuscating, aggravating hag deserves no mercy, my liege. Let's kill her and find that very valuable map I mentioned.*

"I didn't come here for more of your riddles," he said, ignoring the demon but taking note of the moist sheen on the Cartographer's brow. Clearly, she was sufficiently attuned to the blade's magical resonance to comprehend its captive's intent and fear worked to his advantage now. "The last chart you drew for me exacted a high price indeed."

The Cartographer retained enough composure to shrug. "I told you only an innocent could open the box, and in doing so would remain innocent forever. Was it not so?"

Ellipe's face as he stepped towards the ancient wooden chest, eager, bright, trusting…

Guyime's jaw's bunched beneath his beard as he swallowed his burgeoning rage. Scared she might be, but he reminded himself the Cartographer would possess her own defences. "I asked you two questions," he grated, pointing to the map. "I see only one answer."

"You asked me two questions with one answer." Moving with cautious slowness, the woman went to the map, playing a hand across the intricate lines still forming on the parchment. "Fate is what I chart. Your fates were bound in the Execration." Her eyes slipped to Seeker, "Your daughter," they blinked and fixed on Guyime, "the swords you crave, fallen king. To find them you must find her, and to find her you must find them."

Her tone took on a grave, reflective note as she returned her gaze to the map, a sadness stealing over her features. "It's rare, but it happens now and then. I craft a chart that touches one of the old fates, the skeins that wind themselves around history, lines etched into the fabric of the world long ago according to a design I have not the sight nor wisdom to discern. You, both of you, have a very long journey ahead and it starts here," her finger extended to the pictogram in the centre of the Second Sea, "in Carthula."

Chapter Three

CARTHULA

•)———(•)———(•

They left the shop shortly after, there being little else to say, Guyime and Seeker making for the docks through rapidly darkening streets. Lissah stepped out of the shadows when the forest of masts rose above the rooftops, the fishhead dangling from her mouth indicating she had been awaiting their arrival. Lakorath maintained an aggrieved diatribe all the while, his voice shot through with peevish disappointment. *The greatest treasure we could ever have claimed, and you just walk away. Rest assured, my liege, when I find another hand to wield me, it won't belong to such a squeamish ingrate.*

It had often struck Guyime as strange that so ancient a being, one who had perhaps witnessed more history than any other living creature in this world, rarely expressed emotions beyond that of a spoilt and avaricious adolescent. Greed and inexhaustible vindictiveness, he knew, was in its nature, as fundamental to its being as Lissah's liking for fish-heads. Yet, Lakorath couldn't seem to grow beyond his origins. Change, it appeared, was the province of mortals.

The evening tide had swelled and ebbed by the time they reached the docks, compelling them to find lodgings for the night and seek out a berth on a Carthula-bound ship come the morning. A stevedore pointed them to a mean-looking boarding house with an alarmingly slanted roof close to the eastern extremity of the wharf. Guyime deduced the fellow assumed they hadn't the coin for anywhere better.

Seeker paused at the inn's doorway, eyes snapping to the sky at the sight of a solitary bird. It was smaller than the few gulls still wheeling in the air above the harbour, wings blurring as it flew north, a faint but distinctive chirp echoing in its wake.

"He's a long way from home," the beast charmer murmured as the bird became a speck in the overcast gloom beyond the mole. "Slip-wing from the crags south of my homeland," she explained, catching Guyime's frown. "They're clever and never lose the instinct that guides them home, no matter how far away you take them. Some amongst my people would gather great flocks of them, earn coin from passing merchants to carry messages, or protect them from outlaws. They're small but can be trained to attack in swarms. Not a pleasant sight."

A silver and six coppers bought them a room for the night and a meal that was hearty enough if lacking in flavour. Once again, Guyime found sleep beyond him and spent the night seated at the window, his gaze alternating between the street outside and the unfurled map in his lap. The lines were static now but the Cartographer had warned they could change over the course of a journey. *Never forget that it's a chart of fate,* she had cautioned when he took his leave. *And some fates can be avoided. Choices you make will draw the map anew, so choose carefully.*

"Did you believe her?" Seeker's voice was small, coloured by a hopeful note he knew arose from finding the first real clue to her daughter's whereabouts after years of searching. "Ekiri's fate is bound up with finding the swords."

"I'll not pretend to consider her the most trustworthy soul," he replied. "But I saw no reason why she would lie."

"She led you wrong before, didn't she? The innocent hand she spoke of. Who was it? What became of them?"

A boy named Ellipe. He died.

"Best get some rest," Guyime told her. "Long voyage ahead come the morrow and I'd hazard you're not best suited to sea life."

She sighed, accepting his reticence, at least for now. She shifted on the bed, turning her back to him. Lissah lay next to her and she smoothed a hand over the cat's pelt as if seeking comfort. "You should know," she said in a dull voice that told of impending slumber, "I don't care about the swords. However long this journey takes, I'll only ever care about her."

Dusk was fast approaching when the ship brought them within sight of Carthula. Waves blossomed white as they pounded the bases of the dozen huge islets that formed the city, contrasting with the yellow shimmer of the lights scattered atop the sheer slopes rising from the sea, each to a height of at least a hundred feet. As the ship bobbed in the swell and fading light shifted through wind-driven clouds, Guyime gained a sense of monstrous animation from the rearing columns of rock, an impression of something vast and alive frozen in the act of rising from the depths. If so, it had remained immobile for all the centuries it had taken for people to climb its impossible flanks and construct a dense horizontal maze of buildings atop its many malformed limbs. The towering islets were all linked by a matrix of bridges, so many and of such deceptively fragile construction that they seemed to form a net ensnaring a colossal stone prisoner.

Beside him a red-eyed and hunch-shouldered Seeker muttered some form of incantation in her own tongue, probably a prayer of thanks to one of the innumerable beast-gods they worshipped. The voyage from Sallish had entailed ten days of prolonged torture for her, made worse by the grubby, foul-smelling berth they shared in the bowels of the ship. The unseasonably foul weather had seen her unable to eat more than a morsel and liable to disgorge what she consumed shortly after.

"Sailed before," she groaned between bouts of heaving. "Wasn't so bad then."

"Coastal waters are calmer than the deep sea," Guyime pointed out. "And the juncture between the First and Second Seas can be fractious."

Consequently, Seeker clearly viewed the looming city with far less trepidation than he did, if only due to the prospect of once again setting foot on solid ground. "Does the chart give any notion of where to start once we're ashore?" she asked, voice hoarse and head bowed as she held firm to the rail.

"Just a few more lines swirling around its centre." Guyime watched the lights of the city's main harbour grow larger as the helmsman's skilled hand brought them closer. All he knew of Carthula was its fame as a trading port and its legendarily strict laws regarding outsiders. Sailors were not permitted to stray from the docks, visitors allowed only a brief stay and new settlers were forbidden. "I'm hoping it'll prove more helpful once we're ashore," he added, drawing a snort of derision from Lakorath.

The lying bitch sold you a useless bundle of parchment and ink, my liege. If there was anything of worth here I would sense it, and I do not.

Guyime straightened, frowning at what he sensed in the demon's tone. It was coloured by one rarely expressed emotion and another that was completely new: fear and deceit.

"Did you just lie to me?" he asked in a low whisper. "Does something here frighten you?"

I spent the equivalent of a thousand mortal lifetimes serving in the Infernus. What do you imagine could possibly frighten me?

"The Mad God seemed to scare you a great deal. Is what awaits us here worse?"

The demon indulged in a lengthy pause before replying, yet more newly expressed emotions evident in his voice; honest certainty. *I don't know. I do know you should stay on this ship and sail away with the next tide.*

"You've been on my back long enough to know that I don't run from threats."

No. The sword shifted in its scabbard in concert with Lakorath's resigned sigh. *You embrace them, imagining death will be your release from me, no doubt. But didn't it ever occur to you, my liege, there are worse fates than mere death?*

"Two days." The block-faced customs official handed each of them a thin copper disc embossed with the Valkerin symbol for 'visitor'. They had been required to hand over all but a few of their remaining coins to purchase entry to the city, and then only after close and extensive questioning as to their intent. Guyime's story about seeking work as mercenary guards with one of the merchant houses proved sufficiently typical not to arouse any overt suspicion. "No longer," the official added. "Keep to the outer islets. The centre's not for the likes of you and if you're caught there…"

"Ten strokes of the whip and a berth in a slave ship," Guyime finished with a forced smile. "As you said, repeatedly."

The man's frustrated scowl indicated he may have been likely to voice a more caustic reply if not faced with a less imposing figure. "Yes," he sniffed, recovering some measure of self-importance by stabbing a finger at Lissah. "And *that* can't come in. No telling what havoc it might wreak on livestock or diseases it might spread."

"She only kills what I tell her to kill," Seeker said, staring hard into the official's small eyes. "Unless she's especially hungry."

The two armed guards at the official's back straightened as the tension in the small alcove increased. The official, on this at least, was clearly resolute in his refusal and Guyime divined any defiance would involve best-avoided complications.

"Seeker," he muttered, shaking his head.

Her face twitched with the effort of swallowing an insult, not something her people did easily, before she glanced down at Lissah. The cat blinked, hissed briefly at the official then bounded away, swiftly disappearing into the bustle of the docks.

The customs man gave a huff of satisfaction, though felt inclined to utter a final, "Be sure you mind the clock," before jerking his head at one of the guards to unlock the gate sealing off the docks from the rest of Carthula.

"Is this a city or a prison?" Seeker wondered as the gate slammed shut behind them, a key rattling in the lock with swift efficiency.

"It's not so strange for an island realm to protect itself," Guyime said as they ascended a curving stairwell. "Only so many people can live here at any given time. In the northern waters of the Fourth Sea there are islands where it's considered a sacred duty to kill any foreigner who fetches up on their coast."

The stairwell brought them onto a broad, cobbled plaza surrounded on all sides by tall, narrow buildings. They were all of uniform appearance, with shuttered windows and rectangular columns, and constructed from locally quarried stone. The patchwork discolouration of the walls bespoke many years of repair and restoration but the commonality of the architecture was a clear signal that no new buildings had risen here for a long time.

There were people about, mostly traders wheeling their carts to form the daily market. None seemed inclined to converse with two unfamiliar outsiders, although Seeker's painted face drew more attention here than it had in Sallish. Whilst Guyime consulted the Cartographer's chart, she amused herself by glaring back at each curious pair of eyes, causing several curious townsfolk to hurry off, faces downcast.

"It's changed again," she observed, glancing over his shoulder after scaring off an elderly woman with a basket of peaches.

Guyime nodded, seeing how the pictogram representing Carthula had grown in size, taking on more detail and filling a quarter of the available parchment. Curving lines swarmed around it, creating a dense cloud over the centre of the city.

"It seems we are once again obliged to tread a forbidden path," he said, raising his gaze to a gap between the tall buildings where he could see a bridge extending from this islet. It covered a span of two hundred yards to another much narrower stack of rock where it branched off into two. One branch led to a neighbouring islet whilst the other proceeded to the larger, more densely constructed centre. Guyime's gaze focused on the half-dozen halberd-bearing guards clustered at the nexus of the three bridges.

Easy pickings, my liege, Lakorath said, quick as ever with un-asked-for advice. *I reckon I could get them all with just three strokes.*

"We'll wait for darkness," Guyime told Seeker, ignoring the demon. Glancing up, he grunted in appreciation at the overcast sky. "The cloud will obscure the moon."

Lissah crept from the shadows to join them once they took up position in a shadowed doorway close to the gatehouse marking the entrance of the bridge. Predictably, the islet's steep cliffs had provided little challenge to the cat's climbing ability and she preened with a self-satisfied air as Seeker scratched the fur behind her ears. The gatehouse was manned by a guard possessed of an annoyingly disciplined bearing and keenness of eye; however, he proved easily distracted when Lissah burst from the darkened streets to assail his boots with a spurt of foul-smelling urine before letting out a triumphant yowl and bounding into the gloom. The guard's pursuit was brief, if loud in profanity, allowing just enough time for Seeker and Guyime to sprint from cover and vault onto the gatehouse roof before the fellow's sense of duty reasserted itself.

They lost little time in traversing the tiled roof that covered the bridge, moving in a rapid crouch and making it to the nexus point in moments. Wary of alerting the guards with a disturbed tile or two, they lowered themselves to all fours and inched their way around the conical spire that marked the junction. They maintained the same crawl all the way to the bridge's terminus with the central quarter, knowing it would be well guarded.

"Saints' arses," Guyime breathed out the curse as he paused a dozen yards from the end of the bridge. The building that guarded it resembled a miniature fortress rather than a mere guardhouse, complete with arrow slits and crenelated battlements. Several torches blazed atop its parapet and he could see the shadowy figures of at least dozen guards patrolling the precinct below.

"No way past that without being seen," he murmured to Seeker, feeling Lakorath stir in anticipation. "We'll keep to the left of the fort where the shadows are deepest but it'll have to be fight when they see us. Try not kill any…"

He trailed off when she raised an amused eyebrow before shifting to the edge of the roof and casting her gaze down. "Just waking up," Guyime heard her whisper. "Good, means they're hungry."

Her words were soon swallowed by a loud chorus of snicking chirps from below. It soon spread from one end of the bridge to the other, the sound deepening when it was joined by a loud rustling. Guyime began to lean over to spy the source of the burgeoning cacophony then reeled back as the air in front of his face was filled with a mass of leathery wings and blurring, fur-covered bodies.

The bats rose in a dense cloud, spiralling over and around the bridge before descending on the miniature fort in a dark swarm, the shouts of the guards barely audible above the screeching, flapping din. Seeker surged to her feet and started forward at a steady run, Guyime following close behind. They were obliged to leap through the roiling bats to land on the cobbled streets below, Guyime suffering a scratch to his cheek in the process. Catching sight of a guard slashing madly at the swirl of winged rodents, blood seeping from several bites to his face and hands, he considered himself to have gotten off lightly.

They sprinted to a nearby alleyway, drawing up short at the sound of many booted feet echoing through the maze of streets ahead. The bridge guards evidently possessed a swift and effective method of calling for aid. Seeing no alternative, Guyime leapt for the nearest wall, hands gaining purchase on a window sill before hauling himself upward. Seeker, who had been climbing more difficult obstacles since childhood, beat him to the rooftop where he found her holding a hand to Lissah's nuzzling snout.

"She has her ways," Seeker said in response to Guyime's baffled stare. Shaking his head, he hauled himself onto the roof and they began a leaping sprint away from the continuing chaos at the bridge.

"Where to?" Seeker asked. The surrounding cityscape was an anonymous silhouette of spires, angles and chimneys, offering little clue as to a preferred location.

"Somewhere quiet," he replied, whirling his arms to steady himself as he landed on a ledge that turned out to be slightly narrower than expected. Seeker leapt nimbly to his side, delivering a shove to his shoulder that prevented a backward fall.

"There," she said, pointing to a high, richly ornamented spire a hundred paces away. It was the tallest structure they had so far encountered in Carthula, its walls rich in fortuitously deep arches that would provide welcome cover until daylight.

As they neared the spire, Guyime deduced it to be either a temple or a monument, the arches filled with statues of men and women. They all shared the regal bearing and idealised features masons typically reserved for those of divine or royal origins. They had also been fashioned into unrealistically tall and broad dimensions, making it hard to squeeze through to the gloomy refuge beyond.

"Can't you hack a bit off?" Seeker asked, aiming a frustrated kick at the base of a statue. Guyime found himself intrigued by the effigy, finding something commanding in its subject; a woman of austere aspect holding a book in one hand and an astrolabe in the other.

"My days of desecrating fine art are long behind me," he replied, crouching to squint at the lettering inscribed into the statue's plinth. It was Valkerin script, clearly very old from the weathering of the stone and consequently hard to read in the gloom, but he could discern the meaning by probing the marks with his fingers.

"'Trellia Dios Azrallo, Queya and Mother of Wisdom—To move the stars, first you must count them.'"

"What's that?" Seeker enquired, frowning at his murmured recitation.

"A testament, I think," he said, turning to her. "Not a god or a queen. But a person of some import—"

His words died when his eye caught a flicker of movement behind her, the sword thrumming with warning as Lakorath woke to the danger. Guyime surged towards Seeker, dragging her down, the air whistling with the familiar rush of multiple crossbow bolts. They streaked within an inch of Seeker's head to impact on the austere woman's statue. From the way the bolts shattered her face and chest Guyime divined they had been launched from windlass crossbows, probably of the steel variety. No other projectile weapon had so much power, but also no other took so long to reload.

The sword's blade shone bright as it came free of the scabbard, Guyime making a quick count of the craters on the statue before springing to his feet. *Six, launched from the same direction. Sloppy.*

Charging forward, he saw them rise up from a nearby rooftop, tossing their crossbows aside to draw swords. They were all clad in black silks with hoods covering their faces. Guyime took note of the fluency with which they moved over the tiled slopes to meet him, dividing into two groups and fanning out right and left with practiced efficiency. *Not so sloppy after all, my liege,* Lakorath observed. *They know what they're about.*

"But not what they face," Guyime grunted, teeth clenched with the tension of imminent combat. He paused atop a relatively flat section of roofing, allowing the assassins to draw near. One cast some kind of spinning, multi-barbed star at him before leaping to an impressive height, evidently expecting the throw to provide enough distraction for a killing stroke as he descended.

The sword swept left and right, the glowing blade cutting the flickering star from the air before the second stroke sliced the leaping assailant in half. Blood tainted Guyime's face as the bisected body sailed past, the two parts landing with wet thuds on the tiles to either side. Guyime saw four of the assassins immediately abandon their assault but one was already committed, coming in low with his short, curve-bladed sword aimed at Guyime's groin. The demon blade skewered the attacker through the skull before he got within a yard of his target.

Mmm, Lakorath mused in appreciation as Guyime kicked the corpse off the blade and the assassin's blood seeped into the steel. *Nice and clean. No drugs or liquor. More, if you please, my liege.*

The other assassins spread out, letting fly with a barrage of spinning stars which had Guyime dodging and leaping. He rolled over a buttress to crouch on the other side, the whirling projectiles striking sparks as they skittered from the stone. Hearing a tell-tale yowl followed by an exclamation of surprised pain, Guyime glanced from cover to see one of the assassins describing a mad dance across the rooftops, locked in a close embrace with Lissah who had her teeth clamped firmly to his throat. Beyond them he saw another assassin fall with one of Seeker's arrows jutting from his neck.

The remaining two assassins hurled another salvo of stars in Guyime's direction before turning and fleeing. Seeker's next arrow caught one in mid-air as he leapt to a nearby rooftop, Guyime running into her path to spoil her aim as she drew a bead on the only survivor.

"It appears our arrival was expected," he said. "Let's find out by who."

Chapter Four

THE HOUSE OF AZRALLO

◆──◆──◆

The assassin ran and leapt with a speed and precision that told of extensive familiarity with the Carthulan rooftops. His acrobatic fluency made it impossible for Guyime or even the more fleet-footed Seeker to entertain any hopes of catching him. Lissah, however, proved more than equal to the task. Bounding off to the right she became a flicker of red amongst the forest of chimneys, her speed sufficient to place her in a perfect ambush position when the assassin landed beneath the ledge she had chosen. True to Seeker's wishes she restrained herself from delivering a killing bite, instead dragging the man down with her jaws fixed on his shoulder. Guyime was impressed by the assassin's devotion to the circumspection expected of his trade. He bore the cat's teeth and his crushed bones with only a faint grunt, breathing in short but controlled gasps, eyes bright and defiant as Guyime and Seeker came to a halt close by.

"Fast or slow," Guyime said, drawing a dagger and crouching at the assassin's side. "Your choice."

"Pilgrim," Seeker said, voice low and hard. Glancing up, he saw her sinking to one knee and nocking another arrow to her bow, gaze fixed on the hooded figures who had materialised on the opposite rooftop. Guyime counted twenty, all armed with windlass crossbows.

"Fast…" the fallen assassin choked in a harsh rasp. "…or slow!"

Seeker shot a brief glare at Lissah, the cat moving with lethal swiftness to shift her jaws to the assassin's neck, snapping it with a hard jerk.

Guyime risked a glance at the rooftops behind, finding another dozen hooded figures sprinting to cut off any line of retreat. *Been a while since you walked so blindly into a trap, my liege,* Lakorath opined. *But I'm afraid we have more to worry about than a few crossbows.* The sword's blade took on a different colour, the usual blue replaced by a shifting glaze of crimson that appeared whenever it was in the presence of magic.

"Sorcerer," Guyime hissed, sinking lower and moving to Seeker's side. The assassins opposite seemed content to remain in position, making no move to aim their weapons or brave an assault across the gap between the two rooftops. The reason for their lack of aggression became plain when a harsh, chill wind swept around them and Guyime spied the approach of another figure. The new arrival was hard to fully discern against the gloomy backdrop of the sky, but Guyime saw enough to know it moved without setting foot to tile.

It became clearer upon reaching the cordon of assassins, a man in garb that seemed surprisingly mean and lacking in finery for a sorcerer. He wore a hardy coat and boots of leather and carried no staff or trinkets as they were wont to do, mostly for show in Guyime's experience. However, even if he hadn't floated in the air, his nature would have been obvious from the faint green aura outlining his form, signifying a variety of magic Guyime had seen before but thought may now be extinct.

"Y'might want to just come on out," the sorcerer called across the divide, his accent confirming Guyime's suspicions. "It'll make this much easier for all of us." He spoke in the common tongue of the First and Second Seas, but the lilting tones were unmistakable.

A Mareth druid, Lakorath said. *This is indeed a night for novelties. I wonder how he'll taste. You would never allow me to indulge in them, as I recall.*

"Get you gone, druid!" Guyime called back, speaking in the man's own tongue. It had been many years since he spoke it, but the words flowed easily enough since they were often a feature of his worst dreams. "I've no wish to spill the blood of your kind, but I will if you make me! You know what manner of weapon I carry!"

"That I do, fine sir!" the druid called back. "And your concern is truly appreciated. But a man must honour his contracts, else be called a villain, and I'll not have that. Come out now, and let's get this matter settled. I've a ship to board and riches to spend."

"What's he saying?" Seeker muttered in bafflement. "Sounds like a braying goat."

"He's a mercenary sorcerer from the northlands," Guyime replied, sighing in grim reluctance. "And, it seems, too well paid to listen to reason."

She gave a derisive snort. "Then he can listen to this."

Seeker rose before he could stop her, drawing her bow with the skillful swiftness he knew so well, the arrow sure to take the druid in the eye from this distance. A blast of wind propelled her off her feet before she could loose. She collided heavily with a chimney, collapsing senseless to the tiles. Guyime darted forward, using one hand to drag her to cover amidst a blizzard of crossbow bolts, the sword flashing with inhuman swiftness to slice them from the air.

The druid, clearly a man of predatory instinct, lost no more time in idle banter, arcing over Guyime's position at a height beyond any missile he could throw. Roof-tiles fountained as the druid lowered his glowing arms, the gales he crafted forming two miniature tornadoes as they swept towards Guyime and Seeker.

It's a mite higher than we've managed before, my liege, Lakorath warned as Guyime stepped away from Seeker and whirled, sword extended in a two-handed grip. He paid the demon no heed, grunting with the effort of heaving the blade in so tight a circle. He couldn't throw it away, but the experience of trying to had taught him a few additional tricks over the years. Once again, as he put the final ounce of strength into the throw, the handle slipped across his palm for an instant, except this time instead of becoming impossibly heavy, Lakorath allowed the sword to be thrown, albeit with Guyime still clinging on.

They shot upwards, closing the distance to the levitating druid in less than a second, the blade aimed at his chest. He was quick, however, angling his body at the last instant so the sword sliced just his clothing and only scarred the flesh beneath.

Unusual, Lakorath mused, tasting the thin trace of blood which had faded into the steel by the time Guyime landed heavily on a neighbouring rooftop thirty yards away. *Not altogether unpleasant, must be due to whatever magic he carries. But tainted by far too much barley wine for my liking. This one's not fully a drunkard, my liege. But neither is he fully sober.*

The druid's hood fell away as he whirled to face them, revealing the pale features and copper-coloured hair common to his kin. Guyime saw a fierce smile of both pain and appreciation on the druid's face as he raised a bloodied hand from the bleedoing scar on his chest. The kiss of a demon-cursed blade, Guyime well knew, hurt worse than ordinary steel, especially for a practitioner of magic.

"Quite the story you've given me!" the druid called out, floating closer to Guyime. "Another chapter to the epic of Lorweth the Wind Weaver."

"Never heard of you!" Guyime called back, straightening and preparing to whirl again. "Nor will anyone else, before long."

The druid let loose with his gales before Guyime could launch himself into another leap, the twin vortices shattering a trio of chimneys as they chased him from one rooftop to another.

"No need to be rude, my interesting friend!" the druid admonished him between blasts. "Why, there's many a miscreant who consider themselves blessed to meet such a noteworthy en—"

A blinding flash brought an instant flood of tears to Guyime's eyes whilst an accompanying clap of thunder set a very loud bell ringing in his ears. He blinked the water from his eyes in time to witness the spectacle of Lorweth the Wind Weaver enmeshed in a web that appeared to be constructed from threads of pure light. The fierce smile was gone from his features now, replaced by a rictus of agonised rage. The web of light emitted a rain of sparks as it closed around him, singeing skin and hair as it bore him away, resembling a comet as it trailed embers high into the gloomy heavens.

Another thunder clap sounded, not so loud as the first, followed almost instantly by a lightning strike on the rooftop where the assassins still stood. Stonework exploded into powder and flame, two of the assassins tumbling like rag dolls in the explosion. Their comrades turned and fled instantly, Guyime seeing another three caught by further strikes before they disappeared from view.

"Are you hurt?"

The voice came from above, strident with authority, but also coloured by a small note of genuine concern. Guyime tracked the floating figure as it descended, resolving into the sight of a tall woman with long dark hair and a silver band on her head. She wore a long cloak and fine silks of red and blue that trailed in the wind. The clouds above her roiled with fresh energy and a heavy rain began to fall, beading her handsome, bronzed features as she came to rest before him.

Mage, Lakorath said in dark recognition. *Have a care, my liege. I can feel her power and she makes the druid seem like a child.*

"Forgive me," the woman said when Guyime gave no answer, sinking to one knee and bowing her head. "On behalf of House Azrallo, I offer welcome to the slayer of the Mad God."

*S*eeker gave a faint groan when Guyime gathered her up, ignoring Lissah's muted yowl of distress. He followed the mage across several dozen rooftops until they came to a large house with walls that towered over those around it. It was separated from the surrounding streets by a plaza far too wide to be leapt.

"With your permission, Lord Slayer," the woman said, extending her arms to Guyime. "Climbing down will entail a delay and I sense your companion requires a healer's touch."

"I'm not a lord," Guyime returned. "And neither have I slain any gods, mad or otherwise."

A frown of confusion marred the woman's brow. "But we were told of your pilgrimage to the Execration, and were you not once a king?"

"You are well informed, if not entirely accurate."

Seeker shifted in his embrace, letting out a moan that possessed enough pain to banish his misgivings. "I'll tolerate no harm to her," he warned, gently placing Seeker in the mage's outstretched arms.

She replied with a nod and a reassuring smile. "I'll be back for you presently; *she*," she cast a glance at Lissah, smile broadening in amusement at the cat's answering hiss, "can make her own way, I'm sure."

She floated up and over the plaza, bearing Seeker to the mansion swiftly and spending only a brief moment within its wall before returning for him. "Are you sure you can bear my weight?" Guyime asked. The mage had a long-limbed athleticism to her but he was not of typical stature.

"Magic is not born of muscle, my lord," she said, extending a hand which he took after a final twitch of hesitation. He saw her wince as their skin touched, the first glimmer of darkness in her gaze as it snapped to the sword on his back. "Your pardon," she said, forcing another smile, "the touch of demon is never an easy thing to bear."

She bore them both aloft before he could answer, Guyime feeling the hair bristle on his arms and head in response to the magic that enclosed them. It felt like being stung by a million tiny bees at once, a sensation to which he had never become accustomed. They landed on the mansion's roof next to a narrow ornamental pool where a man waited, arms open in greeting. Like the woman, he was clad in red and blue silks, and also matched her height. Guyime saw a clear resemblance in his bronze, high cheek-boned features, their relationship made plain when the woman bowed to him in grave respect.

"Father, I present the Lord Slayer..."

"Such formality, Calandra," the tall man said. "I've a sense our guest has little use for such things."

Guyime's eyes lingered on the man's face for a moment, seeing a great deal of calculation behind his eyes that told of one accustomed to wielding considerable power. Looking away, he cast around for Seeker, finding no one else on the rooftop. "My companion..."

"Conveyed to comfortable quarters under the care of my personal physician." The tall man inclined his head, placing a hand on his chest. "Vatori Dio Azrallo, Queyo of House Azrallo. Welcome to my home." Guyime recognised the word queyo as a modern variant on the old Valkerin term for 'patriarch.' His gaze sipped to Vatori's hand, taking note of the only ring he wore, a large gold band embossed with an astrolabe.

"A descendent of Queya Trellia Dio Azrallo?" Guyime enquired.

"My grandmother and most esteemed of my line." Vatori raised his brows in appreciation. "You are familiar with our history?"

"Only her statue. I'm afraid it requires some repair."

The queyo's gaze darkened considerably, his jaws bunching in suppressed anger as he muttered, "Another crime to punish those Destrino dogs for."

"Destrino?" Guyime asked, but it was Calandra who answered.

"House Destrino," she said as her father fought to contain his seething anger. "A mercantile family with almost as long a history as our own. They are our rivals in certain matters."

"In everything," Vatori said, his voice a little hoarse. Coughing, he mastered himself. "But, let us not sully our first meeting with their name. Come," he turned, extending a hand to a stairwell leading to the mansion's interior, "refreshment and rest awaits."

Guyime didn't move, his habitual suspicion deepened by a vibrant thrum from the sword. *Trust nothing this one says,* Lakorath advised. *Power is his addiction and only passion.*

"I'll have answers first," Guyime said. "Before this day I had never set foot in this city but both you and your daughter seem to know far more about me than I find comfortable. I would know how."

Vatori exchanged a glance with his daughter, neither appearing overly concerned by his intransigence. "Successful commerce," the queyo said, spreading his hands, "is dependent upon the swift transmission of information. A quote from my esteemed grandmother."

Swift transmission... Guyime gave a soft grunt of realisation. Only the Cartographer had known of their destination, and she was in Sallish where Seeker had seen an unfamiliar bird with a talent for always finding its way home. "I hope you paid her a great deal," he said. "She'll need it to hide from me for the rest of her days."

Guyime noticed a certain hardness creep in to join the calculation in the queyo's eyes. Outward affability was clearly matched by inner steel. "The Cartographer and House Azrallo have an understanding," Vatori said. "And enjoy a measure of shared protection."

"Your understanding doesn't seem to include loyalty since she appears to have also sold the same information to your enemies. How else would they know to send assassins and a sorcerer to kill us on arrival?"

"House Destrino contrived to place a spy in my home, a spy who has now been dealt with. I put his head in a box and sent it to his masters not more than an hour ago."

That's true enough, my liege, Lakorath put in. *But I sense there's a great deal still hidden.*

"What do you want of me?" Guyime demanded.

"To honour you as a guest in my home." Vatori once again extended his hand to the stairwell. "Which, according to Carthulan tradition, requires provision of a bed, a feast, and a story, one I am sure you will find of great interest, to our mutual advantage."

Chapter Five

LEXIUS

The slave's eyes bulged behind the thick lenses as they regarded Guyime, reminding him of fish in a bowl in the way they blinked. The man himself was more akin to a rat with his emaciated frame and spindly arms. His slave collar was unusual in being fashioned from leather rather than iron, bearing a brass plaque that bore the astrolabe sigil of House Azrallo. The lenses he wore were fixed over his eyes by three leather straps that swept around his shaven head to meet at the base of his skull. From the callused skin tracing the line of each strap, Guyime divined the lenses were rarely if ever removed. It was impossible to age him, he could have been thirty or fifty. Such was often the way with those who suffered through life.

"Don't gawp, Lexius," Vatori told the slave. "Do you not know you behold a king this night?" His admonition held a gently chiding tone but the immediacy with which the slave lowered his gaze and sank to his knees told of the kind of servility that could only be born from the whip.

Vatori and Calandra had led Guyime through the mansion's descending levels of opulence to a cellar which other such fine houses would surely have given over to the storage of wine. This cellar, however, proved to be a library. Books of varying sizes and bindings lined the shelves that covered every wall, creating a labyrinth lit by only a few carefully placed lamps filled with what Guyime assumed to be glow worm sap. This was a place where even the most meagre naked flame could not be risked. They found Lexius, the slave, alone at the heart of this maze of books. He was standing in expectant and servile respect when they came upon him, evidently having been warned of his master's approach by the echo of footsteps. The slave's desk was neatly arranged with stacks of carefully aligned parchment, the topmost sheets inscribed in dense but neat script.

Guyime was intrigued by the way Calandra moved immediately to the desk, ruffling through the slave's scribblings with careful interest but also not disturbing the neat arrangements. She didn't pay Lexius himself any particular attention, and the small man was assiduous in keeping his gaze averted, but Guyime's experienced eye discerned a certain tense artifice in their mutual lack of acknowledgement.

"I haven't been called a king for a very long time," Guyime said, addressing his words to the slave. "As I suspect you already know. Lexius is Valkerin for 'scholar,' is it not?"

"Or scribe," Vatori said. "Depending on the context or inflection. This Lexius, I'm pleased to say, is both and therefore worth all the coin I paid for him, oh…how long ago was it, Lexius? I forget."

Lexius answered in the respectful but otherwise uninflected tone common to lifelong slaves. "Thirteen years, Queyo."

"Yes, thirteen years. He was even more of an emaciated wretch then, if you can believe it. His old master had him chained to a desk in a dank cell copying out contracts, thirty a day or he'd suffer the whip. A singular waste, for Lexius has a particular talent not commonly found amongst the slave caste, or any other caste for that matter. Would you care for a demonstration?"

Without waiting for an answer, Vatori turned to Lexius. "Relate all known facts regarding the famed northland king Guyime the Ravager."

Lexius began speaking immediately, his words flowing in an unhesitant monotone. "Historians differ as to the exact birth date of the man who would become known as Guyime the Ravager, but most point to some point in the winter of the year 1305, by the Valkerin calendar. Details of his early life remain vague and shrouded in legend, the first credible accounts of his existence as a true historical figure appear in 1324 recording the rewards he received for service in King Orwin the Second's suppression of the Churl's Rebellion. Written testimonials charting his activities grow with each successive year, first concerning his revolt against the authority of the Crown and the Risen Church and the considerable slaughter that accompanied it. The reason for the Ravager's sudden transition to the status of a traitor are opaque, but many chroniclers ascribe it to the arrest, torture and execution of his wife on unsubstantiated charges of witchcraft..."

"Enough," Guyime grated, his tone possessing enough dire warning for the slave to blink his magnified eyes at his master in obvious concern. Next to Lexius, Calandra glanced up from the stack of parchment, flexing her fingers with a cautionary glint in her eye. The moment stretched until Vatori waved a dismissive hand.

"That'll do for now, Lexius," he said. "On that subject at least. So you see, my Lord Slayer, I have a slave who is incapable of forgetting anything. More than that, he understands all that he remembers. Amongst the great many jewels I possess, I own none so valued as he."

Despite his words, Guyime saw no particular fondness in Vatori's gaze as he looked upon his slave. It was a guarded, careful scrutiny, the expression a master of hounds might afford to a prized dog he worries will bite him one day.

"But, I promised you a story," Vatori went on, a fresh smile appearing on his lips. "Lexius, the relevant books, if you please."

The slave bobbed his head and moved carefully around Calandra, still avoiding her gaze whilst she seemed once again fully engrossed in his latest writings. He disappeared into the gloomy recesses of the cellar for a brief interval, returning with two volumes that evidently taxed his threadbare muscles as he heaved them onto the table. The books varied in age, one so ancient its binding was frayed and the script that once adorned its spine no longer legible. The other was of much more recent manufacture with an untarnished leather covering. It bore a title embossed in the modern variant of Valkerin script typically used throughout the First and Second Seas: "House Makiro. Purchase and Breeding Record. Vol. Nine."

"The Cartographer was clear that you came here to answer two questions," Vatori said. "Here lie the answers." He nodded to Lexius who duly opened the most recent volume, thumbed his way to a page and began to read.

"Description: one female, age estimated at twelve to thirteen years. Origin confirmed as the Beast Charmer clans south of the Second Sea. Relevant abilities also confirmed. Value: ten talents of gold. Sale and purchase: confirmed."

Lexius fell to an abrupt silence, stepping back from the desk.

"When?" Guyime asked, advancing towards the slave. "Where?" When Lexius gave no answer Guyime took hold of the book and spun it around. The relevant entry was easy to find by virtue of the fact that details regarding the sale of Seeker's daughter had been carefully excised.

"Tell me who bought her," he instructed Lexius in very precise and deliberate tones.

"He'll tell you only what I permit him to," Vatori said. "Nothing more, nothing less."

Careful, my liege, Lakorath warned, Guyime seeing Calandra flex her fingers once again. He breathed deeply, shifting his gaze from the slave to the master. "I assume you have a price in mind for this information?"

"Of course. All information has a price and this particular nugget took a good deal of digging to unearth. Fortunately, House Makiro's interests were purchased in entirety by House Azrallo some years ago and Lexius had, naturally, memorised their records."

Fortune? Lakorath scoffed. *I think not. The girl's fate is bound to the swords, and so is ours. That map-drawing traitor didn't lie about that, at least. I can feel it now, like a net you can never escape.*

"Which brings us once again to my question," Guyime said, aiming a level gaze at Vatori. "What do you want of me?"

"To tell you a story, as I said." Vatori flicked a hand at Lexius. The slave duly opened the older volume. He was gentle with it; the pages were stiff and dry with age, their edges ragged and the ink that marked them faded into foxed parchment. Lexius leafed carefully through the first few pages, pausing at the title. It had been inscribed by hand rather than printed, this time in old Valkerin rather than any bastardised modern relation: "The

Kraken's Tooth—The Birth of Carthula. A History by Lexius Dius Karnhost."

"One of the oldest books in my library," Vatori said. "And it's still a copy of a copy, the only one known to currently exist in fact. I think we can dispense with much of the text, Lexius. The engravings should suffice to tell the tale."

The slave turned several pages until he came to an illustration. It had faded a great deal and at first glance appeared little more than a grey smear of hatch marks until Lexius lifted one of the glowing jars closer. The image showed a man of classically heroic dimension standing on the deck of a ship, holding aloft an object that blazed so bright it obscured its form. The Valkerin script below the illustration read: "Akrius Doth Claim the Kraken's Tooth."

"Akrius?" Guyime asked Lexius who replied only after receiving a nod from his master.

"The legendary founder of Carthula," he said in his neutral tones. "A Valkerin exile and warrior of great reputation. The legend relates how he escaped with a fleet of followers from Valkeris after a failed revolt and, having been denied harbour in all ports, determined not to allow them to perish on the open sea. With the aid of a spell cast by his lover, the sorceress Tehngrid, Akrius plunged into the waves and dove deeper than any man before to beseech Carthia, the goddess of the oceans, to provide them a home. Seduced by his fabled charm and handsome aspect, the goddess guided him to the corpse of a kraken, an ancient thing of great immensity, devoid of all magic save the glimmer that remained in its heart and just one of its teeth."

Lexius turned more pages, stopping at another illustration. This one depicted the impossibly muscled Akrius standing with his arms folded whilst a man of only marginally less impressive stature raised a hammer above an anvil.

"Returning to the surface with the tooth," Lexius went on, "Akrius had his personal weapon-smith grind it into dust and pound it into the steel of his most favoured sword. Once again beseeching the smitten goddess for aid, Akrius had her awaken its magic by summoning a demon to join with the blade. Thus armed, Akrius returned to the depths and used the sword to cut open the kraken's heart, freeing the magic it contained. So great was the power unleashed that it raised the kraken's bones from the seabed, forming the very islets upon which the followers of Akrius founded their new home, naming it in honour of the goddess who had saved them.

"But, there would be no earthly home for Akrius." The slave's voice took on a faintly sombre note as he turned more pages, the first expression of real emotion Guyime had witnessed from him. The final illustration showed a naked Akrius wading into the waves which had been arranged in such a way as to resemble a pair of expectant eyes. "Forsaking his followers, he went to join Carthia in her domain beneath the waves, for that had been their bargain. Today, when the seas rise in fury and the gales blow ships onto the rocks, it's said to be Akrius raging at his eternal torment, for Carthia, as is the way with gods, soon tired of mortal company and imprisoned the remnant of his soul in the deepest parts of the earth, far beneath the First Sea."

Guyime took a moment to examine the book with his own eyes, finding the few passages he read to correspond to the slave's story, albeit in much more florid and archaic language. "The Kraken's Tooth," he said, turning back to the first illustration. "A demon blade."

"Yes," Vatori agreed. "Just like the sword you carry, the sword that enabled you to survive the Execration."

"The Cartographer's message clearly left out a great deal if you think that's what happened."

"She was fulsome in her report, and the fact remains that you and your companion survived the Execration and the fall of the Mad God, birthing in you an apparently unswayable desire to find a slave girl and the remaining Seven Swords." Vatori came closer, his finger stabbing at the fragile parchment of the ancient book. Guyime heard Lexius stifle an involuntary gasp at the vandalism. "I have found you one of the Seven Swords," Vatori said, voice low and intent. "It lies beneath this city where Akrius left it so long ago, alongside the very heart of a kraken, the heart of this city in fact. Can you imagine the worth of such a thing? Any house that claimed it would enjoy eternal and unchallenged ascendency over Carthula."

Guyime glanced back at the book. "I saw no maps in here."

"There are none. The book in fact contains very little clue as to the heart's location. But these," Vatori stepped back, raising his arms to the enclosing labyrinth of books, "these together form as complete a history of this city as could ever be compiled, every legend, every battle, every marriage, every birth, every cave or tunnel explored, and Lexius remembers it all. *He is our map.*"

Guyime stared hard at the slave, watching his face remain impassive whilst his neck bulged and his eyes blinked rapidly behind his lenses. "Tell me," Guyime said. "And know what lives in this sword can hear all lies. Do you know the location of the Kraken's Tooth?"

Lexius replied instantly, his tone as empty as before but for the smallest croak. "Yes, I do."

No lie, my liege, Lakorath confirmed. *Just a good deal of fear, though perhaps not as much as there should be. I assume you noticed how he and the mage-bitch never look at each other.*

"I noticed," Guyime muttered, his gaze sliding back to Vatori. "I take it you intend for me to retrieve this kraken's heart?"

"And its demon-cursed tooth, don't forget, which you may keep, with my thanks. You will also depart this city with all the information Lexius holds regarding your companion's daughter. In truth, Calandra has been itching to undertake this task herself for a long time but I wouldn't allow it. A father's sentiment, Lexius having compiled a plethora of lurid and precise descriptions of the dangers involved. However, with the wielder of a demon-cursed blade and survivor of the Execration at her side, how can she fail?" Vatori extended his hand, the single ring he wore gleaming dully in the light from the glow-jars. "Carthulans have an old saying: 'A fair deal sells itself.' I believe this deal to be more than fair, don't you?"

He's a very skilled deceiver, Lakorath said in response to Guyime's unspoken query. *Lying about several things at once so it's impossible to discern the truth amongst it all. But it's not all lies. Two things are clear. First, he knows I can detect his deception and doesn't care. Second, he'll see you dead rather than let you take the Kraken's Tooth anywhere. I strongly advise you tell him to find a suitable animal to fornicate with and we'll seek out the sword ourselves. Even then we'll probably have to kill him and a fair number of others before we get ourselves off this benighted rock, if his daughter doesn't kill us first.*

Guyime regarded the queyo's extended hand before raising his gaze to watch the faint smile on his lips remain steadfastly in place. "So, in this city a fair deal sells itself," he said, gripping the hand tight and taking a small measure of satisfaction at the concealed wince on Vatori's face. "Whilst during my reign, a broken deal saw you scourged and hung over a hog-pen with your belly slit open."

He gave an empty smile and released the queyo's hand, turning to Lexius. "When do we leave?"

Chapter 6

THE PORTAL OF WINDS

•)———(•)———(•

"Are you sure of this?"

Much to her annoyance, Seeker's face paint had been washed away by Vatori's healer, revealing the dark, curiously flawless skin beneath. Her features was a little drawn and tense with the after-effects of being rendered unconscious by the druid's magic, but she seemed otherwise fully restored. Seeing her face clearly for the first time had forced Guyime to conclude she was several years younger than he previously assumed, although her people were famously long-lived so it was possible her features didn't reflect her age. Before leaving the mansion she had insisted on daubing her face with a mix of the locally used powders but it was a faint parody of the once-thickly applied mask.

"I'm sure the slave knows who bought Ekiri," Guyime replied, nodding to Lexius. He walked behind Vatori and Calandra at the head of this heavily guarded and well-armed procession, seeming almost childlike in comparison to the armour-plated guards on either side. They were all foreign mercenaries, mostly from the ports on the southern coast of the Second Sea. Numerous scars marred their olive skin and they shared the flint-eyed stare of experienced killers. They were armed with a mix of halberds and steel crossbows which was evidently a popular weapon in this city.

"And," Guyime went on, "I'm sure he's not going to tell us until we find what his master wants us to find."

"And the chart agrees?"

"It's hard to tell," he admitted. "The city fills it now, along with a great many lines that fade almost as soon as they appear. I suspect it means we're close to our goal, if nothing else."

He looked down, noting the empty space at her side. "Lissah?" The cat had failed to make her expected appearance at the mansion and remained conspicuously absent throughout this journey through the streets.

"I warned her to keep hidden," Seeker replied. "But stay close. I remain unsure of our present company…"

She fell silent as the narrow street they followed suddenly opened out into a broad circular plaza. The captain of the mercenary guard, a wiry man with two scimitars on his back and the grating voice of one who has spent a great many years shouting, barked out a command. The guards immediately spurred into a measured trot, dividing into two columns as they spread out to form a perimeter around what Guyime initially took for a large pool in the centre of the plaza. The hour was early and there were few townsfolk about, all of whom rapidly dissolved into the surrounding streets at the sight of the personal guard of Vatori Dio Azrallo.

The queyo and his daughter moved to stand at the edge of the pool which, Guyime saw as he came closer, was in fact a large, deep well of some kind. It was twenty feet across and ringed by a low wall topped with an iron railing, presumably to ward off wayward children or foolhardy adults. To Guyime's eyes the well appeared darker than it should, the brickwork that formed its edges swallowed by a void after only a few feet. Leaning close to the railing to peer down, he found himself blinking in a hard rushing wind from below, his tear-ridden eyes finding no clue as to what lay in its anonymous depths.

"Welcome to the Portal of Winds," Vatori said. He spoke with a clipped urgency, his gaze roving over the surrounding rooftops. "Perhaps the most ancient construction in Carthula, and the entryway to the city's innards."

"What's down there?" Seeker asked, squinting as she peered through the railing.

"A question many have sought to answer for centuries, my lady," Vatori told her, his eyes still scanning the enclosing houses. "Sadly, no one in several lifetimes has ever returned to tell us. A few dozen mad souls climb the railings to throw themselves in every year, but none contrive to climb out again. Fortunately, Lexius has amassed sufficient knowledge to confirm that the portal is not, in fact, bottomless and, once traversed, will lead to the kraken's heart."

"Meaning someone must have climbed out at some point," Guyime said.

"A few, a very long time ago. So long in fact their accounts were buried in various archives and would have remained so but for Lexius and his remarkable memory." Vatori's gaze narrowed and he turned to his daughter, the urgency in his voice increasing. "They're coming, I can smell it."

"House Destrino?" Guyime asked.

"And others. The prospect of one house gaining possession of the heart was bound to unite the rest against us. Calandra…" He trailed off as he met his daughter's gaze, Guyime seeing a certain stricken helplessness in his expression.

"I know, Father," she said. "It's time." Moving with a purposeful but disciplined swiftness, she stepped towards the railing, raising her hands. A brief, blinding flash of light caused Guyime to avert his gaze. When he looked again he saw scraps of glowing iron falling into the gloomy depths and Calandra stepping into the gap she had created.

"We need to join hands," she said, holding out her arms. Lexius moved quickly to comply whilst Guyime hesitated.

"You can carry us all at once?"

"Carry, no," Calandra said. "But I can prevent us from falling." She splayed her fingers insistently. "Please. There isn't much time."

From across the plaza Guyime heard the scrape and shatter of a displaced roof-tile colliding with the ground. The crossbow-bearing guards immediately raised their weapons whilst the halberdiers adopted a fighting stance, all eyes now on the rooftops. Guyime could see no enemies above but had little doubt that a good deal of violence was about to erupt in this plaza.

Stepping forward, he took Calandra's hand, extending his other to Seeker. The grimace on her face as she clasped hands with both him and Lexius, closing the circle, told a great deal of what she thought of this enterprise. However, the possibility of gaining even the smallest crumb of information regarding her daughter was too great to pass up.

The snap and whistle of a crossbow bolt sounded at Guyime's back. Glancing over his shoulder, he saw the guard standing to Vatori's left fall, a bolt embedded in his cheek. Then he was in the air, his feet scraping over the wall as Calandra bore them up. Her eyes took on an opaque, milky sheen as she unleashed her power which proved sufficient to suspend them over the portal for a brief instant before gravity took hold. The hiss of multiple bolts in flight and the shouts of combat rose to a brief cacophony that died as they plunged into the void, stolen by the rushing wind.

The next few moments were a confusion of buffeting air and fast-fading light. Guyime felt his grip on Seeker and Calandra tested by the strength of the gale that assailed them on all sides. He felt them veer close to the stone walls of the portal several times, feeling his skin itch in discomfort as the mage used her magic to prevent a collision. It was as the wind finally abated into a stiff breeze that he began to catch glimpses of their surroundings.

The shaft they plummeted through was lit from below by a pale blue luminescence, revealing rough granite streaked with rivulets of water cascading through innumerable cracks. They fell at a controlled rate that still felt overly fast as the stone slipped by in a blur. When Guyime looked down to take in the sight of a rapidly approaching flat surface he knew instinctively their imminent landing would result in broken bones for all of them, leaving little chance they would ever escape this place.

Fortunately, Calandra possessed a sufficient reserve of strength to arrest their fall at the final moment. The air thrummed with a burst of power as she slowed their descent, allowing their feet to meet rock with only a slight jolt.

Seeker released her grip the moment they landed, unlimbering her bow and reaching for an arrow. She crouched in readiness, peering into the shadowed surroundings in tense expectation.

"Something here?" Guyime asked, recalling her uncanny facility for sensing the presence of predators.

"Something," she confirmed, slowly rising and lowering her bow whilst her eyes continued to rove the shadows. "But, what manner of something..." She shrugged, letting out a frustrated sigh. "I doubt that it's friendly."

They stood upon a slightly angled granite outcrop that jutted into the shaft. The depths below remained as unfathomable as ever but the outcrop led to a ledge with a jagged triangular opening, the interior of which was lit by the faint blue glow Guyime had noticed during their descent.

"Where does the light come from?" he asked Lexius who replied with his usual toneless alacrity.

"At this depth the rock is heavily coated with phosphorus, a mineral that reacts with the air..."

"I know what phosphorous is." He nodded to the opening. "Our next step, I take it?"

The slave nodded but didn't move, instead looking to Calandra. The mage stared upwards at the distant circle of light above. The wind rushing up from below swallowed most of the sound but Guyime caught snatches of discordant shouts and the ring of steel.

"Your father strikes me as a man born to survive most things," he told Calandra, seeing the evident concern in her gaze. "And we shouldn't waste the time he's buying us."

She frowned in reluctance before lowering her gaze, drawing a decisive breath. "The riddle first?" she said to Lexius.

"I believe that would be best, mistress."

She hid it well but Guyime caught the small wince on her face
at his use of the word 'mistress'. *Lie,* Lakorath said. *Whatever she
is to him, she's not his mistress. Raises an interesting question, don't you
think, my liege? In a place where survival depends on knowledge, who
truly holds the power? This rat-faced turd is the master now. I do wonder what might happen when he realises it, assuming he hasn't already.*

"Riddle?" Guyime asked, his gaze shifting between the two
of them in close scrutiny.

"We warned you that the heart is shielded by many dangers," Calandra replied. "The riddle is one of them."

"A riddle set by who?" He addressed his question to Lexius.
Once again, he waited for her nod before responding.

"Accounts vary. Some hold that Akrius crafted them when
he unleashed the power of the heart, worrying what might happen should it ever be disturbed. Others have it that the city's
founders enlisted the help of the most powerful sorcerers of
their time to ensure the heart remain in place forever."

"Then these shields could be no more than legend. In fact,
the heart itself may just be a myth, some malformed rock mistaken for a great treasure by superstitious minds. It wouldn't be
the first time I've seen the mundane revered as divine."

"It's real, my lord." Lexius spoke with a mild tone but Guyime
heard the certainty in it. Whatever the intent of his master, the
slave had no doubts as to the accuracy of his research.

"Call me Guyime," he said. "I've had my fill of titles."

"Well," Seeker said, her gaze raised to the pale circle above.
"He's a hardy soul, to be sure."

A dark shape had appeared in the portal, a shape that resolved into the silhouette of a man floating in mid-air as Guyime squinted at it. "Lorweth the Wind Weaver," he grunted, angling his gaze at Calandra. "Come to settle a grudge perhaps?"

"Or just do his masters' bidding," she returned evenly, flexing her fingers in anticipation. Her mounting agression faded when Lexius moved closer to her, speaking in a voice too soft for Guyime to catch above the rushing wind. Whatever he said was enough for Calandra to give a reluctant frown and turn away, striding towards the opening. "We can't waste any more time here. If the other houses hired one sorcerer, there's a fair chance they hired more."

Guyime followed her through the jagged portal after motioning for Seeker to take up position behind Lexius and guard the rear. The opening led to a winding tunnel bathed in a phosphorescent glow that banished all shadow, leaving just various shades of blue. It instilled a sense of unreality, as if they had stepped into a separate realm far removed from the realities above. "This contest to claim the heart seems curious to me," Guyime said as he followed Calandra. "Since your city's survival supposedly depends upon its presence."

"The heart will remain in Carthula, regardless of who claims it," she replied, moving with a surefooted swiftness he assumed to be the result of having memorised a route set down by Lexius. "Possessing the very thing upon which Carthula was founded has been the ambition of every great house for generations. This contest, as you call it, has been looming for a long time, like an ancient trap waiting for something to trigger its spring." She glanced back at him briefly, her eyes made dead and unreadable in the blue light. "Which, it transpires, was you."

"And what will your father do with the heart when he claims it?" Guyime persisted. "Usher in a new age of peace and prosperity for all Carthulans?"

"Are you really in a position to preach morality, your highness? Lexius has taught me a good deal of history, so I know your story and found little evidence of peace in any of it."

"Then you'll know what I'm likely to do in the event of a betrayal."

"Yes." He caught a faint curve to her lips as they rounded a corner. "The same thing I would do, I expect. So, let us proceed warmed by the light of our mutual understanding."

Different, Lakorath observed. *Now she's out of her father's sight. It wouldn't surprise me if his is not the only agenda here, my liege.*

Chapter 7

THE RIDDLE

•)———(•)———(•

The tunnel's glow lessened somewhat as they proceeded, the passage eventually coming to an abrupt
halt where it met a ledge less than a yard across. Below
lay a chasm, its depths lost to the shadows, whilst the gap
between the ledge and the flat expanse of stone beyond was
spanned by a bridge. It was constructed of two elegant arcs
of stone, meeting at the summit of a massive rough-hewn
pillar that rose from the void below where it widened to
form a platform.

Guyime's gaze was soon captured by the spectacle of
the granite wall opposite the platform which had been fashioned by means unknown to resemble a giant human face. It
would probably have retained a noble aspect but for the deep
crevices decades of dripping water had carved into its surface. Consequently, the visage that confronted them as they
crossed to the bridge's central platform appeared to be that
of a scarred, agonised victim to some dread wasting disease.
The impression of a soul in pain was heightened by its open
mouth, as if frozen in mid-scream.

"Akrius?" Guyime asked Lexius.

"Most likely." The slave's eyes narrowed as he surveyed the stone features, blinking in recognition as they tracked upwards. "There's an inscription carved into the forehead. I believe it to be archaic Valkerin but the lettering is too worn to fully transcribe." He looked to Calandra. "Mistress, if you could…"

She raised her arm, fingers splaying to emit a stream of lightning from each fingertip. However, instead of striking out the bolts floated away, twisting and entwining to form a bright ball of luminescence. Calandra kept her arm outstretched, guiding the ball towards the face then up so that it threw the lettering etched into its heavy brows into stark relief.

Guyime had sufficient knowledge to translate most Valkerin text but the unusual grouping of the characters and unfamiliar phrasing made this a difficult message to decipher. Lexius, by contrast, did so in mere seconds.

"Ahhh." The slave let out a soft exhalation of satisfaction. "We have our riddle. 'I soar yet have…'"

His voice was drowned out by a large thunderous rumble from above, the din accompanied by the grind and squeal of heavy metal. Dust cascaded from the cavern's roof along with several large boulders as the vibration displaced loose granite. Guyime felt the platform tremble beneath his boots and worried for a moment that this ancient bridge might be about to fall, then it stopped.

Silence reigned as they exchanged glances, Seeker allowing a rare smile of relief to play over her lips. The smile, however, soon widened into a shout of alarm as a whooshing noise came from the shadows to their front, accompanied almost immediately by an identical sound to the rear.

A huge crescent-shaped blade came sweeping out of the gloom, fixed to the end of a lever the size of a tall pine. Guyime whirled in time to see another swing out of the shadows behind. They impacted the right and left spans of the bridge simultaneously, cutting through both like steel through paper.

Guyime crouched amidst the explosion of grit and shattered stone, the impact of the dual axes sending slabs of granite tumbling into the chasm. He watched the two huge axes reach the apex of their swings whereupon they paused. It was only a brief hesitation, however, accompanied by the sound of grinding metal as hidden gears adjusted somewhere in the roof of the cavern. Then the axes swung again, sweeping down to destroy another portion of the already sundered bridge, this time shearing away stone less than ten yards from the central platform. The axes swept up and paused again. More grinding of unseen machinery then another downward swing, this time close enough for Guyime to make out the symbols etched into the somehow rust-free steel that formed the axe-heads.

"Delvian spell-script," he said. "There's more than just mechanicals at work here. Don't waste your strength," he added when Calandra raised a hand, presumably intending to cast her bolts at the axes. "The spells will ward off sorcery."

"The demon-blade," she said, nodding to the sword handle jutting over his shoulder.

"Won't work either." He turned to Lexius as the blades completed their next sweep, grunting in discomfort when a chunk of shattered stone bounced off his shoulder. "The riddle!"

Lexius's eyes blinked behind his lenses for a heartbeat and Guyime was gratified to see them free of panic. The slave waited for the axes to swing again, grimacing at the sting of a stone splinter scoring a cut on his shaven scalp, before speaking with an untroubled fluency.

"I soar yet have no wings. I cut yet have no blade. I kill yet no hand wields me. What am I?"

"Soar yet have no…" Guyime's muttered repetition died as the axes impacted once more, this time slicing into the central platform itself. It shuddered under the impact, forcing him to consider how long the pillar they stood on could withstand a continued battering.

"The wind," Calandra said. "The wind soars and kills." She turned and shouted at the great stone face. "The wind!"

The axes swung up, paused for their typical momentary adjustment, then plummeted down once more, sending Calandra off her feet and rolling perilously close to the edge of the platform. Moving with a lithe swiftness Guyime would have thought beyond him, Lexius sprang to her side, reaching out to clamp both hands to her flailing arm. He drew her back fractionally before the next axe swing descended. Guyime knew that for a slave to touch his mistress without permission was an offence usually punished by death, but seeing the shared expression of deep relief and gratitude between Calandra and Lexius, knew instinctively that such restrictions did not apply to their relationship.

Triumvirate's balls, Lakorath muttered with a faint note of disgust. *It truly is blind after all. Mortals are such contrary characters.*

"The riddle!" Guyime hissed in reply. "Some demonic insight would be welcome at this juncture, unless you relish the prospect of lying at the bottom of this chasm for the next few centuries."

I don't know. The sword shifted a little in the manner that told of a shrug. *Perhaps try it in Valkerin?*

Guyime surged to his feet, shouting the Valkerin word for wind at the stone visage. "Saero...!"

The axes bit deep into the platform, sending him sprawling as they cut away a section a yard wide on either side. Guyime calculated they had at most two more swings before the inevitable and grisly result. A burst of heat and sparks came from his left where Calandra's desperation caused her to put his theory regarding spell-script to the test. The lightning shot up to envelop the axe blade on their right as it reached its apex, shimmered then faded as the great lever swung once again without noticeable pause.

"Saero!" Guyime yelled again before quickly blurting out every word for wind he could recall. "Alsish! Hekrehan! Jekarmah..."

His voice died as the four of them pressed together, the axes passing within a foot and birthing a dense cloud of powdered rock. When it faded they stood upon a column barely five paces across. The next swing, he knew, would leave nothing except some bloodied chunks of meat tumbling into the dark.

"It's not the wind," he said, looking again at Lexius. The slave's face was tense with concentration, the skin on his forehead forming many creases as the brain within sorted through his prodigious memory. As the ominous grind of gears sounded once again the slave's brow smoothed and he looked up to regard Guyime with large eyes, full of both sorrow and shame.

"I don't..." he began, voice fading amidst the whoosh of descending blades.

Seeker's bow thrummed, Guyime's gaze snapping to track the shaft as it described a shallow arc before disappearing into the wide, screaming mouth of the great stone face.

A booming echo reverberated through the cavern as the two axes came to a juddering halt, each no more than an arm's reach from the platform. Dust and fragmented stone descended in concert with the thud and clatter of mechanicals coming to pieces, then both axes fell, plummeting from view in a cloud of debris.

"An arrow doesn't have a blade," Seeker said as she lowered her bow. "Also, no hand wields it when it kills."

She glanced around at the yawning gap between the platform and the nearest ledge. "Does anyone have a notion of how we're going to get off this thing?"

Chapter 8

THE WAGER

C alandra conveyed each of them in turn to the flat expanse of rock on the far side of the chasm, though her increasingly wan complexion and sunken eyes indicated the effort had cost her.

"We should rest a while," Guyime said. "Let you recover your strength."

"There's no time." She cast a wary glance back at the great stone face, now partially obscured by the gloom. "The other houses' hirelings will be coming, their pursuit made easier now that we've cleared the first obstacle."

"They may take a different route, mistress," Lexius said. "The route to the heart is not a straight line." To illustrate his point he nodded to the two broad fissures in the rockface ahead.

"The Wager or the Maze." Calandra's features tensed in uncomfortable indecision. "Neither appeals greatly at this moment."

"The Maze always struck me as the more hazardous. Though neither should be regarded as lacking peril."

"It might help," Seeker put in with a hard note of annoyance, "if my friend and I had some notion of what you two were babbling about."

"The Maze is…" Lexius's wiry frame moved in a shrug, "…a maze, as the name suggests. Successfully traversing it requires certain difficult choices."

Seeker raised an impatient eyebrow when he fell silent. "Such as?"

"The accounts are unclear as to their exact nature. But one phrase does recur: 'Choices no soul would ever wish to take.'"

"And the Wager?" Guyime enquired.

"Also shrouded in mystery, except, of course, that a good deal of chance is involved. Also, a malevolent ghost of some description. Some say a witch, others a mighty hero from antiquity."

"The sword can banish all ghosts." Guyime moved to stand between the two fissures. "And it's always best to take the surest course. Which way to the Wager?"

They were only a few paces along the right-hand tunnel when Guyime saw Seeker stiffen again, taking on the familiar tension that told of a threat. "The same something?" he asked.

She nodded. "The same. Stronger now, more…present. Were we in my homeland, I'd say we just crossed into a rock lion's favourite hunting ground…" Her voice trailed away when they rounded a corner and the blue glow of the tunnel shifted to a more vibrant, green-tinged luminescence. More arresting than the change in light, however, was the sight that lay beyond the tunnel's mouth.

"You are seeing this too, aren't you?" she asked Guyime in a low murmur.

"Sadly, yes."

It was a young spruce, only ten feet or so in height, its trunk rising from sun-dappled green grass, branches outstretched to the rays of light streaming through a lush forest canopy. Small birds flittered amongst its leaves whilst butterflies bobbed above the many bluebells that surrounded its roots.

"An illusion," Guyime said. Despite the pleasant scene he found himself unwilling to take another forward step.

"An illusion wouldn't hold a scent," Calandra said, Guyime catching the perfume of grass and flowers on the gentle breeze.

"Besides," the mage added, moving past him to step free of the tunnel, "I would know a glamour, and this isn't one." She strode towards the spruce and ran a tentative hand over its trunk, a half smile appearing on her lips. "As solid as you or I."

Moving with great caution, Guyime emerged from the tunnel to take in their surroundings. The forest began a dozen paces away, all manner of trees spreading out in a dense thicket to fill his field of vision. Looking up, he saw a blue sky scattered with cloud and no sign of the expected cavern roof.

"From dreams she wove her domain," Lexius murmured, sunlight gleaming on his lenses.

"A quotation, I assume?" Guyime asked.

"Carthia was not just the Queen of All Seas," the slave replied. "She had been cast out of the Divine Realm by her father, Herthis, when he became enraged by her many dalliances with mortal kind. He condemned her to the chill of earthly oceans in the hope it would cool her boundless lust. Before that she had been the Goddess of Dreams and Fables and even in her exile retained the power to recast the waking world into whatever she wished. A few legends recount how she crafted a domain for Akrius in the belly of the kraken."

"Clearly she had an eye for beauty." Calandra spread her arms out as she stepped beneath the shade of the trees, a laugh escaping her lips. "So long since I saw a forest, though I never saw one like this."

"Have a care," Seeker warned, maintaining her tense crouch as she scanned the forest's many shadows. "Pretty it is, but it smells wrong."

Guyime was about to ask Lexius for the route to the Wager but paused at the expression on his face as he watched Calandra twirl beneath the trees. Even distorted by the lenses, Guyime could easily recognise what he saw in the slave's eyes.

Told you, Lakorath chimed in. *Sickening, isn't it?*

"How old was she?" Guyime asked Lexius. "When her father bought you?"

Lexius immediately averted his gaze from his mistress, head lowered in subservience and mouth set in a straight, unspeaking line.

"Not much older than you, I'd guess," Guyime persisted. "They say the mage-gift is dangerous when it first manifests itself, requiring careful tutelage and guidance to ensure it doesn't destroy its bearer. Even as a child, I'd guess you still knew a great deal, enough to help her, perhaps?"

Lexius's eyes flicked to him before focusing on the deepest shadows of the forest. "I suspect the Wager won't be far away," he said, striding off.

Disrespect to a free man, Lakorath mused. *Worthy of a flogging at least, but he doesn't seem overly concerned.*

"No," Guyime agreed, following as Seeker and Calandra began to trace the slave's steps. "Only a slave who considers himself already free or already dead fears no punishment."

As Lexius predicted, the site of the Wager was quickly found, if hard to recognise at first.

"Too clean," Seeker said, peering at the skull with a critical eye. "It should be darker if it's been here long enough for all the flesh to rot away."

The skull lay atop a rectangular marble plinth some four feet high, staring up at them with empty eyes that offered no clue as to its origins or purpose. Guyime could tell it had belonged to a man of impressive size from the thickness of the jaw and brows.

"Five," Lexius said, crouching to part the foliage covering the lower part of the plinth, revealing the Valkerin numerals carved into the marble.

"Another one here," Calandra said, pointing to a second skull and plinth a few paces away. Seeker found three more as they spread out, soon coming to the realisation that the skulls, six in all, had been arranged in a circle. Each plinth was inscribed with a consecutive number in Valkerin script. The circle enclosed a small clearing, distinguished from the verdant forest by the pile of leaves that covered it, all an autumnal shade of bronze.

"One to six," Guyime mused to Lexius. "Numbers in a game of chance?"

"But what game?" Calandra wondered. "And what are the stakes?"

Lexius's brow creased as he moved from skull to skull, Guyime seeing how his magnified pupils narrowed as his mind churned the various possibilities. Finally, after prolonged consideration, he moved to the plinth inscribed with the Valkerin symbol for 'One' and touched a hand to the skull it held.

The wind rose as soon as his hand touched bone, the sky above the trees darkening to roiling grey and black clouds as branches creaked and groaned, the leaves covering the clearing whipping into a copper spiral. Guyime felt a familiar itch as the wind chafed his skin; the touch of magic, but different from Calandra's aura, possessing a disconcerting harshness bespeaking a very different wielder.

The buffeting wind faded to a stiff and chilly breeze as the last leaves were scoured from the ground, revealing a jumble of bones. They were piled atop one another in haphazard fashion, ribs and spines interlaced with skulls and thigh bones. Unlike the skulls sitting atop the plinths, these exhibited the cracks and stains of natural decomposition. Guyime caught the gleam of various ancient trinkets amongst the piled remnants.

"So," a voice said as a figure shimmered into existence in the centre of the remains. "I am to be plagued by yet more fools from the world above."

The figure was seated on a chair fashioned from bone, legs and arms fused together to form a parody of a throne. It was hooded and bent, two spindly grey-skinned hands emerging from the sleeves of its mildewed robe to clutch at the armrests of its obscene perch. The face within the hood was lost to shadow but the voice that emerged from it was female. Guyime was struck by the lack of a croak when it spoke, finding it possessed of a strength and authority normally heard only from those possessed of great wealth or privilege. It was a queen's voice, but laced with an unconcealed air of knowing condescension as well as deep bitterness.

"Come to try your luck, have you?" the figure enquired, its head rising a little to reveal a sliver of the pale, ancient features within. "What are you this time? Heroes in search of the power to topple tyrants? Or just another gang of greedy rogues?" A sigh that resembled a tired dog's rasping bark emerged from the hood as one of the spindly hands flicked fingers at the surrounding carpet of bones. "You'll find them all here. The brave and the cowardly, the mighty and the weak. Take a long look and ask yourself if you'd really like to join them. If the answer is no, please be so good as to piss off and leave an old woman to her rest."

Guyime exchanged a quizzical glance with Seeker. "She doesn't sound much like a goddess," the beast charmer whispered. The seated ghost, however, clearly possessed very good hearing.

"Because I'm not a goddess, you stupid bitch."

She leaned forward on her corpse-throne, revealing more of her face, a creased, bloodless mask resembling dried paper but still somehow retaining an echo of regal handsomeness in her lofty cheekbones and narrow nose. "Do you want to play or not?" she demanded, her hand making spidery progress from the armrest to the folds of her robe. When it emerged Guyime saw a die resting in the leathery palm. "Only one of you, mind. And, just so you know, bet wrong and you will all join my congregation."

"I'll take your bet," Guyime said, stepping forward secure in the knowledge that, should the game go against him, the sword would shield them from the consequences.

"Not you, you tall streak of piss!" the ghost snarled. "I choose the player. It's the only joy left me in this eternal punishment." Her eyes tracked over the four of them, narrowing in calculation. "I ask a question and whoever answers it gets to make the wager, except you, piss-streak. I know the nature of that thing on your back and don't think I'm letting it anywhere near me.

Not you either." She flicked a dismissive hand at Calandra. "Too much magic in your veins." Her gaze narrowed further as it switched to Seeker, pursing her cracked lips in consideration. "Beast-charmer, eh? Been a long while since I caught sight of one of your lot. A potent gift you have, one I'm immune to but your tribe always had plenty of other tricks. You!" She stabbed a bony finger at Lexius. "Feeble body. Let's see if you have a feeble mind to match."

The ghost settled back on her throne, rolling the die between her thumb and forefinger. "Tell me, what is my name?"

The answer came quickly from the slave's lips, spoken with his customary uninflected fluency. "Tehngrid."

The ghost's fingers froze. It was some time before she spoke again, her voice suddenly dull. "Four centuries since someone got it right. I was starting to think I had been utterly forgotten in the world above. So, my feeble-bodied friend, what do they say of me now?"

"Your story is found only in old books and scrolls," Lexius replied with the same lack of hesitation. "It changes with the teller and the telling. You were either Akrius's concubine or his wife. You were the daughter of a mad Valkerin emperor or the orphaned bastard of a brothel slave. All, however, agree that you were a sorceress of great power and every account of your life ends with the founding of Carthula."

"Just faded ink on dusty parchment, eh?" Tehngrid's ghost let out a small, empty laugh. "That's what I earned, is it? That's my reward for devoting my life to a just cause. Know this, my learned wretch, Akrius was neither my husband nor my lover, I had others for that and I was never particularly discerning. My gifts gave me beauty and a long life to enjoy its benefits. What

Akrius gave me was a dream, a vision of life beyond mere indulgence. A vision of a free empire where none knew the weight of chains or the sting of a whip. That's why I followed him, and this is what it brought me."

She reclined in her throne, gesturing to the bones and the surrounding forest. "Carthia's blessing, or curse. I'm not sure which for her ways were ever mysterious. It could be what she thought I wanted, for gods do not understand mortals any better than we understand them."

"What did you want?" Lexius asked, his voice now laced with a rare emotion Guyime recognised as hunger. After a life spent in study of ancient and often nebulous legend the scholar-slave was now faced with a deep well of answers to a great many questions.

Tehngrid's face once again slipped into shadow, her form taking on a stone-like stillness. When she spoke again, all Guyime could hear in the voice that emerged from her hood was the bitterness from before.

"I am not here to educate you, wretch. You are here to wager. I am here to watch you fail and punish that failure, as the goddess ordained." She raised a hand and crooked a finger. "Come on, then. Best get it over with."

"Lexius..." Calandra said as the slave stepped onto the carpet of bones, crushing an ancient ribcage underfoot.

"It's perfectly all right, mistress." Lexius paused to offer her a brief bow then continued forward, snapping old bones with every step towards the ghost. She waited until he came within a few paces of her throne before holding up a hand.

"The rules are simple," she said, waving at the circle of plinths and the skulls they bore. "You roll the die. The number it gives you matches a number on one of these plinths. Each skull once belonged to a comrade of mine. They were brave and noble and in life, but death has made all but one cruel and vengeful." She held out the die. "Roll, and choose."

"And when I've chosen?" Lexius asked.

Tehngrid's head shifted again, revealing the smile on her lips. "Hope it's the only kindly soul, even though it never is."

Lexius nodded and duly held out his hand, the ghost dropping the die into his palm. Closing his fingers over the ivory cube, he stepped back lowering his gaze to the carpet of bones. His face wore the mask of tense concentration Guyime knew signified a considerable intellect at work.

"Two thousand and forty-eight," he said finally, glancing up at the ghost.

"What?" she asked in irritation.

"The number of people who have come here to wager over the years. This amount of bones equates to a total of two thousand and forty-eight. Do I miscalculate?"

Guyime saw the smile on the ghost's lips morph into a resentful sneer. "I don't keep count. They come here, they irk me with their dull-witted questions, they choose a skull and its previous owner comes to life and kills them, every one a victim of their own greed or ambition. I couldn't give a rat's turd for how many."

"It's impossible," Lexius stated, holding up the die. "Two thousand and forty-eight throws of a die, six possible outcomes with every throw. It is impossible for every throw to have resulted in the player's death. You have been cheating. Unless, there never was a game with rules to break." He lowered the die, focusing his fierce insight on her half-shadowed features. "How exactly did your shade come to reside here?"

"That," her lips drew back from teeth the colour of tombstones, her tongue flickering like a black snake, "is not your concern. Roll."

"Why?" Lexius raised an eyebrow in apparently genuine curiosity. "There's no point. There is no wager that can be won here. No kindly soul to discover. No game orchestrated by a goddess. This is a sham, a means by which you indulge your cruelty."

"Roll, you mortal filth!" Tehngrid lunged forward, hands clutching the throne like claws as she barked out the command, eyes shining with a predatory lust Guyime had seen on the faces of many a sadistic soul.

Rat-face is right, Lakorath said. *She's lying. All she wants is to watch people die. A diverting pastime for a caged soul, forever denied release.*

"Pilgrim," Seeker murmured, hefting her bow. He followed her gaze to the nearest plinth. The skull sitting atop it seemed to have acquired a fresh covering of vines. However, as the tendrils spread, glistening, to cover the skull from jaw to crown, he realised they were in fact muscles and tendons. The skull rose and bobbed as the new-grown flesh doubled in size, white bone shining amidst the red and grey as a spine and ribcage grew to add form to the obscene assemblage. A brief scan of the other plinths confirmed each skull was rapidly being absorbed into a new body.

"How did you come to be here?" Lexius demanded of Tehngrid, throwing the die at her hooded face. "What did you ask of the goddess?"

The ghost's only response was a wailing snarl, a sound echoed from the throats of the skinless bodies slipping from the plinths. They screamed in hate-filled hunger as they lurched on half-grown feet towards Lexius, raising clouds of shattered bone, moving with preternatural swiftness despite their unfinished state.

Seeker's bow thrummed, sending an arrow through the neck of one glistening figure but it barely seemed to notice the wound, continuing to charge, reaching out to the slave with clawed hands of bone and bare muscle. Calandra spoke a rapid incantation, raising her arms to cast out a torrent of lightning. Guyime had already gained a marked appreciation for the power she could wield, but still found himself daunted by what she unleashed in this moment. White bolts coiled around three of the shambling figures, tearing them into shreds. She halted the flow of magic for a brief second, rushing to Lexius's side before blasting apart the other three figures, now fully grown. Guyime managed to gain a full view of one before the white fire claimed him, a great tall man, marvellously muscled with the kind of broad, handsome features he thought were only found on statues commemorating long-dead heroes.

Calandra's fire faded as she focused her glowering visage on the seated ghost, lips moving in another incantation before she swept out then in, the bolts forming a scythe of blinding light. They came together, releasing a blast of blinding energy that forced Guyime to shield his eyes. When he looked again he saw the ghost of Tehngrid still sitting on her throne of bones.

A shade is already dead, Lakorath pointed out. *You can't kill what doesn't live and magic won't banish an earthbound spirit.*

Guyime expected Tehngrid to voice a defiant laugh, perhaps cast a few choice insults at her ineffectual tormentors. Instead, he was confronted with the sight of a slumped and weeping old woman.

"Nothing..." he heard her sob as he strode across the carpet of bones. Her hooded head shook and her shoulders heaved with every sorrowful gasp. "Countless years in this prison and now..." Her head came up, the hood falling away to reveal the creased and decayed mask of her face. "Now you have left me nothing!"

Her anger dissipated as quickly as it had risen, Tehngrid once again subsiding into forlorn weeping. "I begged her to give him back to us," she whispered, voice finally riven with the croak previously absent from her queenly tones. "We stole our way into the kraken's belly, giving everything to free him. All for nothing. We wandered for days without food, with only acrid, poisoned water to drink. They all died...leaving me alone to beg Carthia for salvation, for Akrius to return. She came to me at the end. So...beautiful. So cold. She watched me die then captured my soul here. Kindness or cruelty. Who can say? When others came centuries later, seeking the heart and the tooth, I would help them...at first. But they always failed, and each time they seemed smaller, less and less worthy of the treasure they craved or the help I offered. I began to hate them, and hatred breeds cruelty."

She fixed a tired, empty gaze on Lexius, voice becoming dull once again. "So, that is your answer, learned wretch. That is how I came to be here. And here I will remain with even cruelty denied me."

Lakorath sent a tremble of disquiet through the sword as Guyime drew it from the scabbard, the blade's glow flickering in reluctance. Lakorath had never liked the taste of ghosts.

"It won't end me," Tehngrid said, shifting her gaze from Lexius to Guyime. "I doubt even a demon-cursed blade can overcome the will of a goddess."

"This blade can sever all bonds," Guyime assured her. "Divine or not." He raised the sword in a two-handed grip, preparing to swing.

"Wait." He saw a change come over her then, the lined, strained features transforming into the woman she had once been, as handsome and perfect as any statue. "To claim the heart and the tooth requires sacrifice. The greatest sacrifice. Know this and…" He saw gratitude glimmer in her flawless eyes for a second. "And know the thanks of an undeserving soul."

Tehngrid's shade let out a shriek that mingled pain with exultant relief as the sword cut her from shoulder to hip. The throne beneath shattered as the sword completed its swing, the shade's scream fading as its two constituent parts slipped into tendrils of coiling smoke soon borne away into the depths of the forest by a stiff wind. Trees swayed in the sudden gale, the sky above unleashing a torrent as it turned black, but instead of water, it rained dust. The forest gave voice to a vast sigh as it sublimed away, every tree, bush and leaf falling into the powdered remnants of the stone from which it had been crafted. Within a few seconds all that remained were tall dark dunes, glittering in the glow from the cavern walls.

Chapter 9

THE MAZE

◆————◆————◆

"**S**acrifice," Guyime said to Lexius as they inched their way along the ledge. "What did she mean by that?"

The journey from Tehngrid's cavern had entailed crawling along a narrow channel of damp, uneven rock that eventually opened out onto a ledge barely a foot wide. It traced away into the hazy gloom, following the sheer walls of a subterranean canyon. They had been making a slow but steady progress for close on two hours now with no end in sight.

He saw the slave's shoulders stiffen a little in response to the question but his tone had recovered its usual neutrality. "I don't know."

Not a lie, exactly, Lakorath reported. *But there's something... deeper. A kernel of insight he doesn't want to acknowledge.*

"All your studies," Guyime persisted. "All those myths and legends, and none made mention of sacrifice?"

"Not in any significant way."

It was only a fractional movement of his shaven head, just a small glance at Calandra as she cautiously navigated a corner a few yards on, but Lakorath caught the scent of its meaning clearly.

Fear, my liege. He's scared, and not for himself. It's my opinion that he'll happily sacrifice you and the beast-charmer, and anyone else for that matter, in order to save his lady love. Let's not forget the lengths her father went to embroil us in this farce. Were it not for the knowledge in his rat-shaped head, I'd advise pitching him into the depths of this abyss.

The ledge broadened after another hour of careful progress, separating from the canyon wall to form a downward-slanted viaduct. It sloped towards the mouth of a huge cavern, its unnaturally flat surface riven with a matrix of winding channels, each wide enough to allow passage of one person at a time.

"The maze," Lexius said as they came to a halt.

Scanning the labyrinth, Guyime saw that its exit point lay in the shrouded recesses of the cavern, making it impossible to memorize a way through. "Lead the way," he told Lexius who replied with an apologetic grimace.

"There is no lead I can offer," he said. "All the legends were clear on this; we must each choose our own path."

"How?" Seeker asked. "To make a choice you have to be given a reason."

Lexius replied in a tone that indicated another quotation plucked from his prodigious memory. "'And lo did they traverse a labyrinth crafted from their own sins, for Carthia was ever given to ruminating on her misdeeds and it amused her to see mortals suffer the same pain.'"

Seeker cast a sour glare at the maze. "I'm starting to greatly dislike this goddess."

A scream from the rear caused them all to whirl as one, Seeker reaching for her quiver whilst Guyime's hand grasped the sword. Peering into the canyon he saw no immediate threat, but his ears did detect the scuff of many boots on stone.

"One of House Destrino's hirelings must have lost his footing," Calandra concluded. She lowered her hands, turning to start along the viaduct. "I've sins enough for plenty of choices."

They moved across the viaduct in a steady run, pausing at the sight of the single gap in the wall of stone they found at the end. The maze had many paths but only one entrance. An echoing shout from behind convinced Guyime there was no time for further consideration and he strode towards the opening, pausing when Seeker placed a hand on his arm.

"Sins," she said, her gaze full of wary tension. "I have many, but you…"

"None I don't face whenever I have the misfortune to dream." He forced a smile and stepped into the maze.

The first thing he noticed was the change in the air, the chill mustiness of the cavern abruptly replaced by a less redolent but far colder atmosphere. His breath misted and his fingers began to numb as he cast about, noticing another salient facet of his new surroundings: he was completely alone.

Glancing back at the expected sight of the opening, he saw only smooth stone, glass-like in its sheen and lack of flaws. Turning away, he found the surrounding walls casting a darkened, shadowy version of his own image back at him.

A maze of mirrors, my liege, Lakorath mused. *Irksome to be sure, but hardly the stuff of nightmares, for most. But not you.*

"Shut up," Guyime snapped, starting along the passage, his footsteps birthing long echoes. Turning a corner a few paces to his left he found himself presented with a junction. Two separate passages branched off to left and right; what lay beyond both remained in shadow until he came closer. The scents came to him first, a mix of woodsmoke laced with the hunger-inducing aroma of cakes on the skillet emerged from the passage on the left. From the right came the decidedly less pleasant sting of wet straw, horse dung and unwashed people.

The combination of smells summoned the memories almost instantly, springing to the forefront of his mind with such clarity he knew what he would see even before the shadows shifted into grey cloud and began to swirl, taking on discernable form. To the left he was presented with the sight of a boy about ten years old peering through the open doorway of a kitchen. The boy's eyes were lit with the hunger known only to children as they tracked the progress of the honey cakes from the cook's skillet to the plate where they would be left to cool. Guyime knew this kitchen and this cook. He also knew well the boy and the crime he was about to commit.

The scene to the right was far uglier, but still he found he preferred it. A thin man of besmirched appearance stood on a cart with a noose about his neck. His eyes had an over-bright, unblinking aspect and his tongue licked continually over the partially dried blood streaming from a recently broken nose. The cart and the dray to which it was tethered stood beneath a H-shaped frame in a courtyard, strewn with hay in a vain effort to mask the odour of dung from the horses that regularly traversed its cobbles. Guyime recalled that it had rained that day, making the dung reek worse than usual, but the rain and the stink hadn't discouraged the mob. Fully three score people had come to stand witness. Their faces, only marginally less besmirched than that of the man on the cart, were lit with a peculiar anticipation that resembled the greed in the eyes of the boy from the kitchen. But whilst he hungered for cakes, they hungered for the sight of death. His father had been a fair man but sparing in the entertainment he provided his churls.

Guyime watched two men-at-arms in the grey and blue livery of House Mathille toss the rope over the wooden frame whilst a tall bearded man in the garb of a minor baronet read aloud from a sheet of parchment.

"What is done here today is done under law of Church and Crown!" Guyime's father intoned. He spoke with a fluency that indicated familiarity with the script, but law dictated it be read from parchment bearing the king's seal. "Know that on this day we name Bolthal the Hedge-man, known commonly as Bolt Hedge, a villain. Know that this man stands accused and convicted of sundry crimes, most grievously the murder of his wife, Goodwoman Astrith, formerly a maid of work in this very castle on the perfidious and false claim that she lay with another man in contravention of vows. Know also that several witnesses have attested to the numerous occasions on which this man profaned the Saints and failed to do proper obeisance on appointed days of rest and worship. Having done required penance under priestly observation and willed restitution of all worldly goods in equal part to Church and Crown, the sentence of castration and disembowelment has been commuted to merciful death by hanging."

Piers Mathille, Baron of Falthon Castle and head of House Mathille, lowered the parchment to turn a stern and commanding visage upon the boy standing at his side. The boy was taller than his younger self from the kitchen, his face taking on the hard lines and prominent chin that would distinguish him in adulthood. But any manly aspect was negated by his evident fear, the tears he tried unsuccessfully to banish from his eyes and the trembling of his hands as they clutched a horsewhip.

"To your duty, Guyime Mathille," his father said, nodding at the cart.

The image froze as Guyime's twelve-year-old self stared up at his father, face stricken and eyes imploring. He recalled what came next with terrible ease, his father's anger at his son's public display of weakness and the hard refusal to allow him to shirk this task. In a moment he would lower his gaze in shame and walk towards the cart on stumbling feet, keeping his eyes averted from Bolt Hedge as he mumbled his last mostly incoherent prayers to the saints. The whip would crack sharp in the air as it flicked the dray's rump, causing the beast to lurch forward. His father would whisper a harsh order to watch as Guyime stared at the shit-covered ground, and watch he would. Bolt Hedge took a long time to die that day, and the mob took full pleasure in his passing.

Not much of a choice, Lakorath observed. *A theft of cakes versus the first time you killed someone. From what I gather, to successfully navigate this maze you must suffer through your sins. It appears you'll have to witness the hedgeman's death all over again, my liege.*

"It wasn't my first killing," Guyime said, turning to the passage on the left. "Nor the greater sin."

The memory began to unfold as soon as he stepped into the kitchen, the fragrant warmth that once brought sighs of pleasurable anticipation now summoning a shudder. He watched his boyhood self wait for the cook to gather up a basket and make for the larder. Scurrying to the plate, the boy smothered a yelp as the first touch scalded his fingers, but nevertheless proceeded to cram a cake into his mouth. They were his father's favourites, baked specially every morning, and foul would be his temper if they failed to arrive at table. This was as much a prank born of jealous resentment as a crime of greed. Young Guyime gathered up his jerkin and upended the remaining cakes into it, continuing to munch on his spoils as he swiftly departed the kitchen.

Well, Lakorath drawled, *that was dramatic.*

"Father knew what I'd done, of course," Guyime said. "He always knew. But when the cook reported the theft the blame fell on her maid, one Goodwoman Astrith, an unmarried girl of sixteen years with no surviving family to take her in when she was cast out of the castle. So she took up with a hedge keeper from the town below the hill, a man of notoriously foul temper and unreasoned fits of jealous rage. He hacked her to death with a billhook because she smiled at a passing soldier."

Guyime closed his eyes, long-buried guilt summoning a brand of pain he hadn't known he could still feel. "I said nothing. Made no admission to spare her disgrace. Father had me stand at his side when he dismissed her, knowing all the while what I had done. Perhaps he hoped I would speak up, confess at the final moment. But I think he knew I wouldn't. Of all the many disappointments I heaped upon his shoulders, that may have been the worst. Killing her worthless shit of a husband was bad, but it at least brought the satisfaction of sparing the world the presence of a murderer, for it's not his face that haunts me, it's hers when she cried and swore to all the Saints she had never done a bad thing."

So, one crime breeds another. An inescapable, if tiresome truism of mortal kind, one your father seemed keen for you to learn. You must have hated him a great deal.

"For a time. But in the end, long after he died, the hatred faded. For I knew by then that he, despite his many flaws and the delight he took in judging mine, was still a better man than I."

The kitchen slipped briefly into shadow, then Guyime found himself back in the narrow passage with its glass-like walls. The way behind had sealed shut and ahead lay a long doorless corridor, long and straight, narrowing to a distant point with no corners. This maze was apparently a living thing, but kept alive by what?

By the goddess, of course, Lakorath replied as Guyime started forward. *This whole place has the stink of the divine on every nook and cranny. But it's old, so very old and I sense no godly eyes upon us. It's like a clock, wound up and set to tick away the years, crushing those foolish enough to find themselves caught in its gears.*

"Don't you ever tire of your own insights?"

By the Triumvirate's mighty balls no! I'm by far the most insightful person I've ever met.

He came to the next junction after what felt like a mile or more of steadily plodding along the unerringly straight corridor. This time the scene to the right showed a version of himself over a decade older than the boy in the courtyard, clad in armour stained with red and black evidence of recent battle. He stood alongside a row of other armoured men, each one raising their swords in a reverse grip, blades pointing down at the exposed necks of the bound prisoners kneeling at their feet. They wore mean clothes and scraps of scavenged armour, some bleeding from recently suffered wounds and soon to die in any event. In the background their piled weapons were rich in scythes, wood-axes and sundry farming tools.

The aftermath of the Churl's Revolt, I assume? Lakorath enquired. *Slaughtering captive foes, my liege. Hardly the act of a hero.*

"The king named it a traitor's field," Guyime replied. "No mercy was to be shown. I didn't relish it. Hated it, in fact. But, still I did it. Those rebels knew the stakes when they began their uprising. Defeat would bring only death, quick if they were lucky, slow if they weren't. These were the lucky ones. Their leaders took days in the dying."

Once again, the less gruesome scene to the right proved to be far harder to witness. A young woman with honey-coloured hair sat in a bed, her knees drawn up to her chest, a blanket only partially covering her naked form. Her face was drawn in sorrow but even that couldn't diminish her beauty, but then nothing ever could in his eyes.

"You don't have to go," Guyime heard her say, his heart lurching at the sound of her voice, a voice he hadn't heard in the waking world for many long years.

"I can't," he whispered, eyes closed tight. "Not this."

The maze has its rules, Lakorath reminded him. *Follow the worst of your sins.*

Forcing his eyes open, he stepped into the bed chamber, heart thumping as his long-dead wife spoke on. "Your father would send only money whenever the king called a muster, and never suffered for it."

Loise Mathille, newly married Lady of Falthon Castle, stared up at him with verdant green eyes, the legacy of her Mareth blood, even though her family were two generations removed from their homeland. She spoke the northland tongue with no accent, dressed as custom and church dictated, observed all laws and offered nothing but kindness to every soul she met.

None of it would save her when blight took the crops and the town priest, as desperate and starved as his flock, fixed upon her supposed Mareth witchcraft as the cause of all their ills.

The memory of the day Guyime returned from war to find her burnt and barely recognisable body tied to a pole in an ashen pyre was a terrible thing he could never escape. But this was worse, for this was his first betrayal.

"It's different this time," he said, speaking the same lie he had told her. "The king wants swords, not coin. The churls are poor in arms but rich in number."

In truth, the missive delivered by the king's messenger had included a proviso for payment of twice the usual stipend from any knight too infirm or beset by pressing local matters to march under the royal banner. The cost was high, but his father's will had been surprisingly generous. It would have been a relatively simple matter to gather up a few dozen churls and pack them off to the muster with his sergeant-at-arms and a suitably large purse. But then he would have been denied the chance at glory that only came with battle, glory that might win him royal favour, perhaps even a grant to extend his lands. This Guyime had been an ambitious young man.

It was only a small shift in Loise's green eyes, accompanied by a slight creasing to her brow, but he knew she had heard the lie in his voice. Once again he endured and resisted the impulse to confess his dishonesty, crave her forgiveness and promise he would never allow war to take him from her side.

"Then may fair winds and clement skies mark your journey, my lord," she had said, forcing the smile expected of a loyal wife. "And hurry back, for I sense our many children are keen to be born."

The scene slipped away into darkness and Guyime found himself on his knees, forehead pressed against the chill and unyielding stone wall of the maze. When Lakorath voiced his inevitable taunt, he could only bob his head in miserable acknowledgement.

Your pardon, my liege, the demon said. *But I find myself compelled to observe that you were truly a fucking idiot.*

Guyime placed his hands against the wall and slowly pushed himself upright, turning to regard yet another impossibly long corridor. His sins, it appeared, were not yet exhausted.

I'm curious, Lakorath went on as Guyime began a stumbling forward progress. *What did you do to the priest?*

"He had a family," Guyime muttered back. "A mistress and two bastards, though it was forbidden by church law. Hypocrites are often found amongst clergy. I locked them in his chapel and made him watch as it burnt down. He was lost to madness by the time I took his head. I carried it on my saddle for the first few weeks of my rebellion, until its stench began to irk me and I threw it in a ditch. I had plenty of others to replace it by then."

How delightful. Perhaps that's what we'll see next.

"No. We won't." Guyime's feet tripped as the wave of dread and guilt swept through him, causing him to stumble into the wall, drawing up short at the distorted face that stared back at him; the face of a man riven by terror. He felt a sudden temptation to slump to the floor, huddle into a ball and lie there until thirst and starvation took him. Better that than face what he knew waited up ahead.

Get up, Lakorath instructed with unusual curtness.

"You don't know…" Guyime breathed. "You don't understand."

Understand what? That you're as vile a mortal soul who ever trod this benighted earth? That I already know, my liege. I also understand that if you succumb to your self-pity and perish in this maze, I am likely to lie here for as long as there are gods in the heavens. Now, get on your feet and start walking!

The face in the walls' distorted mirror blinked, Guyime seeing grim acceptance replacing the terror in his eyes. He deserved this pain, he knew that, and more besides. He rose, taking a deep, shuddering breath, then resumed his walk with as purposeful a stride as he could muster.

It took longer this time, mile after mile of dogged traipsing along an arrow-straight channel that felt more and more like an elongated dungeon. When it ended there was no junction to greet him, just one last shadowed portal that faded to reveal a scene he had been expecting with every step. The sight still brought a groan to his lips, however, though he forced his eyes to remain open.

"I thought it was supposed to be a library," Ellipe said, hopping up onto one of the tables, thickly laden with dust like all the others. "All I see is boxes." He jangled the ancient lock on one of the chests crowding the table before hopping onto its neighbour, moving with a surefooted litheness that had served him well in his short but dangerous life.

"It's an archive." Guyime's lips moved in concert with the words of his unseen younger self. "Not quite the same thing. Stop pissing about and help us look."

The others stepped into view then, the most loyal and long-serving retainers to the exiled rebel baron who pretended to kingship. Leonne, the Knight of the Kindly Hand who had been so disdainful of Juseria's gilded statue, sallow features bunched as he prodded various boxes with a tentative finger. Sir Julean of the Great Sword, standing taller than any man Guyime ever met, casting his doleful eyes over the dust-covered clutter of this place. Ihlene with her jet hair and scarred brow, forcing interest onto a bored face as she joined the search. He had always suspected her loyalty stemmed from an expectation of frequent battle rather than true sympathy for his crusade against the Risen Church. All thirteen of them, scouring the old vault the Cartographer's map had led them to, all but one as damaged and filled with violent spite as the man who led them, and it was the only innocent soul who found the box.

"Isn't that it?" Ellipe asked after skipping onto another table, pointing to a box otherwise unremarkable amongst all the others but for its length and narrow dimensions. The image shifted as Guyime's younger self stepped closer to inspect the boy's find. Unlike many of the chests in this archive, this box had no latch and no lock, its only decoration a small carved symbol visible under the dust that covered it.

Guyime's hand wiped away the dust to reveal the symbol in full, a symbol in script he couldn't read and would later learn was beyond the comprehension of all mortal eyes. *My sigil!* Lakorath exclaimed in delighted recognition. *So long since I saw it, oh, must be a thousand years or two ago. I had a bunch of woad-spattered savages in my thrall in those days, they would carve it into the foreheads of their defeated enemies...*

Guyime barely heard the demon's wistful reminiscence, his attention focused entirely on Ellipe's wide eyes as they stared up at him, pleased to have won approval from the man he had followed for so many difficult miles. Pleased, unsuspecting eyes. The eyes of an innocent, in fact.

"Should I open it…" Ellipe began, time slowing to a crawl as he spoke the final word, the sound elongating into a grating echo, "…Father?"

What? Lakorath said, abandoning his self-absorbed reverie.

"Ellipe Fitz-Mathille," Guyime replied in a flat, empty voice. "Bastard son to Guyime Mathille, the Rebel Baron, later known as the Ravager. His mother was a serving wench from the town's better tavern. A kindly soul of quick humour and generous spirit, generous enough to take the lord's fifteen-year-old son into her bed one night when the ale had flowed a tad too freely. Father knocked me halfway across the room when he found out. Tupping a wench was one thing; insisting on acknowledging her bastard was another. But I held to it, despite the beating and the threats of disinheritance. He was my blood, Mathille blood, like it or not. So, he was taken in and his mother sent off to the capital with a fat purse. Generous she was, but motherhood was not in her nature. Father insisted the formal acknowledgement be kept secret until his death, so shamed was he. So we pretended my son was an orphaned recipient of the lord's generous heart. But everyone knew. Loise knew, and loved him like her own brother, and me for never pretending he was anything other than my son. When the priest raised the mob against her he fought them, just a boy of ten against dozens, and was nearly beaten to death for his pains."

For once, Lakorath had nothing to say.

Guyime's gaze returned to the box and its unreadable sigil. "I asked the Cartographer for the means to complete my crusade, and she gave it to me. All I had to do was open the box to claim it. Only an innocent hand could undo the wards that had kept it contained for five centuries, and who could be more innocent than Ellipe?"

And in opening it, remain innocent forever, Lakorath recalled. *You must have known what it meant.*

"I knew what it could mean. I hoped it meant he would be the same kind, brave soul for the rest of his days, spared the bitterness and vengeful hatred of his father. But I knew... In my heart I knew what it really meant."

Time resumed its flow as Ellipe, always keen to please his father, began to pry the box open. "Leave it!" Guyime barked, as he had all those years ago. But it was too late. Ellipe was too brave, too curious and too addicted to his father's approval.

There was no flash of sorcerous light when his deft hands pried the box open to reveal the untarnished sword within. No thunderclap of unleashed ethereal energy. Ellipe let out a small breath and stiffened, his eyes rolling back in their sockets, his death coming so swiftly he was denied even a final glance at the father who had proven himself so unworthy of his love.

Guyime screamed as he caught his falling body, crushing his small frame against his chest as if trying to imbue his corpse with the hammering of his father's heart. He howled in anguish, he roared in grief and self-loathing, and through it all knew himself the most wretched of liars. This was always going to happen, for he had loved Loise more than he loved Ellipe. This was the first truth the demon-cursed blade had taught him: vengeance requires sacrifice.

Chapter 10

SACRIFICE

•)———(•)———(•

The maze had vanished when he raised his gaze from his empty arms, fresh tears dampening his cheeks and dewing his beard. Sitting back on his haunches, he drew air into his lungs in hard sobbing gasps, awareness of his surroundings dawning only slowly. He knelt on a flat expanse of bare rock leading to a broad tunnel that echoed his diminishing sobs back at him.

"Pilgrim?"

Seeker's sandals made a soft scrape as she moved to crouch at his side, Guyime turning to regard her face. The powder that adorned her features had been smeared into a garish mask, although the tears had already dried. He saw concern in her eyes and wondered at her facility for quelling her own anguish to have a care for his, for surely he deserved no such concern.

Looking over his shoulder, he saw the maze sealed shut, just a long blank wall of smooth stone. He took a small crumb of satisfaction at finding Calandra and Lexius had also survived it, although the journey had clearly left its marks. The slave stared at his mistress with a new uncertainty to his gaze whilst she kept her eyes averted from him, arms folded in a tight, defensive embrace. Whatever sins the maze had forced them to endure, clearly they related to each other.

"Was it...bad?" he asked, turning back to Seeker.

A momentary pain passed over her face before she drew back and got to her feet, proffering a hand. "Bad enough. We should move on."

"Is there any urgency now?" he wondered, taking her hand as he hauled himself upright, jerking his head at the blank wall behind. "I doubt there's many hirelings willing to face that."

As if in answer to his words a loud crack reverberated through the air as a deep fissure appeared in the wall's surface. More cracks followed with unnatural swiftness, within seconds the wall becoming an abstract matrix of interlocking flaws. There was the briefest pause, then it all collapsed at once, causing the three of them to shield their faces from a thick pall of dust and grit. It cleared quickly to reveal a curious landscape of jagged stone, rising like tall glass thorns from the cavern floor. A difficult field to traverse, but certainly not impassible.

"Served its purpose now it's done," Guyime murmured, taking some satisfaction from the destruction of something that had, in effect, been a vast torture device. He turned to the others, raising his voice and gesturing to the way ahead, the flat expanse of rock taking on a noticeable slant a hundred paces away before descending into the gloom beyond. "If the tooth and the heart are now in reach we shouldn't waste time in claiming them. Unless," he paused to raise an eyebrow at Lexius, "there are more trials to complete?"

"No." The slave exchanged a charged glance with Calandra before starting towards the slope. "There should be no more trials now."

"Except the sacrifice the ghost spoke of," Guyime reminded him as they followed Lexius onto the darkened slope, Calandra falling in on his left whilst Seeker took up the rear.

"Yes," Lexius said in faint agreement. "Although, it could be said we have already sacrificed a great deal in this enterprise."

Guyime saw Calandra stiffen at his words, her reply possessing a sullen note but also a desire for understanding. "I was a child," she said. "Spoilt, indulged…"

"'Don't buy that one, Father,'" Lexius cut in, Guyime quickly realising he was quoting words heard in the maze of sins. "'He looks like a rat. Buy the other one…'"

"I am not that child any longer. And you are not that slave."

"They made us fight!" Lexius halted to round on her, teeth bared and eyes blazing in the only expression of anger Guyime had seen from him. "His name was also Lexius, for what is the point of giving different names to slaves? We would call each other One and Two. He was my only friend. They whipped us until we fought each other. I bit his throat open, all so my master would have a chance to sell me to your father. Because, it transpires, his brat preferred one over the other and it amused him…"

"I'm sorry!" Calandra spat the words out through tears, staring at him with wide imploring eyes. It was enough to silence Lexius, his anger leeching away into a grim resignation.

"We came here to win freedom," he said. "For both of us, remember?"

"Of course I remember."

"Then know that my first act as a free man will be to unchain myself from you."

He turned away and walked rapidly down the slope, deaf to the tearful pleas Calandra cast in his wake.

The slope broadened as it descended, the rough walls of the cathedral-sized cavern that enclosed them fading away, replaced by comparatively smooth stone formed into a great bowl. The nadir was shrouded in shadow for much of the climb, but as they drew nearer Guyime caught a flicker of gleaming metal and the speckled sheen of what appeared to be wet rock.

The gloom was deeper here; the phosphorous that provided light in this underground domain was absent from the bowl's confines, meaning the only luminescence came from the cavern roof far above. Guyime scanned the featureless slopes, finding no recesses or crevasses where a threat might lurk. Despite the reduced chance of ambush, he noted how Seeker's tension had returned. She moved with an arrow nocked to her bow, ensuring every step was carefully placed whilst her eyes continually roved the shadows.

"I recognise it now," she murmured when she caught his questioning glance. "From the Execration."

"A demon?"

She shook her head. "The Kraken's Grave. We've found another. Older, and far more deadly."

It was then that Guyime felt a change to the air, the chill dissipated by a warmth that faded after a few seconds before returning once again. Peering at the glimmer of metal and the

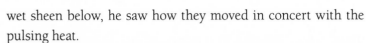

wet sheen below, he saw how they moved in concert with the pulsing heat.

"The kraken's heart still beats," Lexius said, his previous anger now supplanted by awe.

The heat grew in intensity as they neared the heart, Guyime seeing flares of red within its swelling form with each pulse. It stood about a dozen feet high and twice as long, its lower reaches seemingly atrophied into rock whilst its upper side retained the veins and glistening tissue of a living organ. Jutting from its side, within an arm's reach of his head, was a sword.

Half the blade was buried in the heart and the meagre light glimmered on the exposed blade and hilt, both remarkably untarnished. Guyime recognised it as a Valkerin short sword, the famed stahlius that featured on so many ancient statues and relief carvings of legions on the march. It was unadorned but for a symbol embossed onto the pommel, the Valkerin 'A'.

"Akrius," Lexius breathed, reaching up towards the sword's handle, as he did so, Lakorath let out a wordless shout of warning and Guyime's hand shot out to snare the slave's thin wrist.

Don't touch that thing! Lakorath instructed. *Within it lurks no ordinary demon. It's sated by the kraken's animus for now, but the taste of a mortal soul will draw its gaze to us, and you don't want that.*

"Touch it and we all die," Guyime said in response to Lexius's frown, releasing his wrist. "Or so I'm told." He reached over his shoulder to draw his own sword, addressing his next words to Lakorath. "How do we claim it if we can't touch it?"

You don't. You leave it here and scurry away hoping it fails to notice our visit.

"It's what we came for. I won't leave without it."

The sword buzzed angrily in his grip, the blade emitting the greyish blue glow that signified Lakorath's frustration. *Some mad soul contrived to place a nehmavore in that thing,* he stated with forced patience. *A third rank demon that feeds on the souls of the dead or the dying, and it's been feasting on the soul of a kraken for a very long time. That's a great deal of power for one demon and I doubt it'll take kindly to being woken from its glutted torpor. We need to get out of here.*

"Feeding?" Guyime's brows creased in puzzlement. "The legends say the Kraken's Tooth cut the heart open to release its power."

Then these legends, as is often the case, are full of shit, my liege. The sword didn't release anything, it contained it. It was thrust into the heart of a being of immense power that had been dying for centuries, preventing what soul remained from slipping away. This city wasn't built on the unleashed magic but an imprisoned soul. The sword is the lynchpin that holds this place together. Remove it and you'll bring the whole rotten edifice down upon us.

"What is that thing saying?" Calandra demanded, scowling at Guyime's blade.

"That this entire journey has been a fool's errand," Guyime sighed, looking again at the stahlius as it rose and fell in response to the heart's mighty pulse. "Unless he's lying. He does that sometimes."

And you always know when I do, Lakorath pointed out, his blade glowing brighter. *Am I lying now?*

Guyime's sigh became a growl as he shifted his gaze to Calandra. "The demon that inhabits the Kraken's Tooth will eat the soul of any mortal that touches it, and drawing it free will most likely destroy the city above too. That's the sacrifice Tehngrid warned of."

Calandra stared helplessly at the stahlius before shifting her gaze to Lexius. "So it's not what we thought it was. But there's still power to claim here, and am I not powerful too?"

"Don't even think of it," Lexius stated.

"You trust the word of a demon?"

"No, but I trust the word of the man forced to bear a demon's company for a lifetime." The slave's former anger had disappeared now and Guyime saw only naked love and concern in his face as he reached for Calandra's hand. "There are other routes to freedom. Other means to break chains..."

"Chains, is it!?"

The voice echoed from above, rebounding around the great stone bowl with disconcerting volume. Torches flared to life on the slopes, forming a circle of flame. Guyime counted forty in all, his eyes catching the gleam of the weapons they bore, most notably the steel crossbows carried by many.

"I've got chains too, y'see?" Lorweth the Wind Weaver's voice possessed a conversational note as he stepped through the circle of torch-bearing mercenaries. His progress down the slope was accompanied by the chink and scrape of iron links as he dragged a slumped figure across the stone.

"Not yet," Guyime told Seeker, hearing her bowstring begin to creak. Sparks blossomed on Calandra's fingertips as she turned to face the druid, but soon died at the sight of the chained figure's face as Lorweth dragged him into the light cast by the heart.

"Let's have no more unpleasantness, now." The druid slackened the chains in his grip, allowing Vatori Dio Azrallo to stumble onto all fours, his bloodied face dripping black beads onto the stone. "I'm instructed to offer you a quick death for this nasty bastard," he paused to deliver a sideways kick at Vatori's gut, "and half a day to get out of the city, and you can feel free to take your ratty pet with you. All you need do, darlin', is stand aside. You too, my interesting friends," he added, waving a dismissive hand at Guyime and Seeker. "All nice and civilised, wouldn't you say?"

"Impressive scars," Calandra observed, nodding to the burns visible on Lorweth's face, a testament to their last meeting. "Would you like some more?"

The surrounding circle of mercenaries tensed as she flexed her fingers, birthing a fresh cascade of sparks.

"Careful now, darlin'." Lorweth tightened the chains, drawing a pain-filled moan from Vatori. "You're a fair hand with the lightning sure enough, but rest assured I can draw out all the air from yer da' so fast he'll be choking on his own lungs before the first bolt singes a hair on me head."

"Calandra…" Vatori's voice emerged as a harsh, grating gasp, eyes glistening as his captor allowed him to crawl forward an inch or two. He stared up at his daughter in unabashed desperation, but also a firmness of resolve, a particular kind of resolve Guyime had witnessed only a short time ago. "Do nothing…he says!" Vatori blurted. "Claim the tooth! Kill them—"

"That's enough now, da'!"

The queyo's words choked into a gargle, eyes bulging as Lorweth drew the chains taut once more. The druid bared gritted teeth at Calandra, speaking with forceful sincerity. "Enough of this palaver. Stand aside or watch him die!"

Guyime watched her lower her hands, her gaze slipping from her father's bloodied face to Lexius. The slave's eyes were wide and beseeching behind his lenses. "There are other routes to freedom," he said, reaching for her but Guyime could read her intent as plain as day.

"Don't!" he hissed as she tensed. "He's lying."

She met his gaze with a hard determined gaze, though he did see a flicker of a smile on her lips. "I have been given no other choice."

"Not the druid, your father. This," Guyime waved the glowing sword at the surrounding mercenaries, "it's all farce. Theatre. The fight in the square, the pursuit, all lies to force you through the trials and get you to this point." He shifted his focus to Vatori, seeing a new resentment creep over his face. "Tell her," Guyime said. "Tell her how you orchestrated it all. Was it Lexius who uncovered the truth about the sacrifice needed to claim the sword? No, I don't think so. It's something you learned long ago, perhaps from the Cartographer or another greedy peddler of arcane knowledge."

"Lies!" Vatori spat. "Pay no heed to this lying monster, Calandra! Save yourself! My life matters not..."

"He knows you won't run," Guyime cut in, turning back to Calandra. "He knows that sacrifice is required to claim the sword and the power it keeps contained. But he's not sacrificing himself, he's sacrificing you."

To his surprise he saw no shock on her face, nor anger, just a slight broadening of her lips as she cast a sad but contented smile at Lexius. "I know," she said. "I have for quite some time. Apologies, Father, but I'm bound to inform you that there is at least one soul in this world far more clever than you, and infinitely more deserving of what I do now..."

"NO!" Lexius lunged towards her but she was already whirling away, her hand clasping the hilt of the Kraken's Tooth and drawing it free of the heart.

Air rushed from Guyime's lungs as a wave of released power erupted from the heart, casting him high. He tumbled through the air and would have been thrown further if Lakorath hadn't imbued the sword with its anvil-like weight. It plunged straight down with sufficient force to pierce granite, cracking it open and raising a dense cloud of powdered stone. Guyime landed on his feet, but the impact was still jarring enough to send him to his knees.

He looked towards the bowl's nadir, finding it now bathed in a reddish glow emanating from the heart. Its stone-like underside was rapidly returning to flesh whilst the mighty organ beat with increasing rhythm, seeming to swell with every pulse and sending a shudder through the stone beneath Guyime's feet. He expected to see Calandra's corpse lying beside the heart, sword in hand, but she remained upright, still gripping the stahlius as it flamed white and blue. The blade shuddered with blurring energy, Calandra staring into its glowing depths, gaze furious and determined, her teeth gritted against the agony of combating demon magic with her own.

"The sword!"

Guyime's gaze snapped to the sight of Vatori scrambling to his feet, his chains falling away as he directed a commanding shove at Lorweth's stunned and recumbent form. "Get me the sword!"

The druid sat up, shaking his head before taking in the sight of Calandra's furious struggle with the demon-cursed blade. His gaze didn't linger long before he got to his feet and turned smartly about, casting a farewell over his shoulder as he hurried up the slope. "Sorry, yer queyo-ship, but this is far beyond the scope of our agreement."

"Kill him!" Vatori barked, waving his arms at the circle of mercenaries, his gaze alighting on Guyime as he did so. "And that one!"

Guyime saw Lorweth cast a hand at a pair of mercenaries, his gales sending them tumbling up and over the edge of the bowl as he maintained an unbroken stride up the slope. The hard snap of a bowstring sent Guyime into a crouch, tearing the sword free of the stone and whirling to watch a mercenary drop the crossbow in his hands, raising them to scrabble at the arrow jutting from his throat. Beyond him, Seeker smoothly nocked another arrow to her bow and loosed it at the closest enemy.

Guyime ended the agonies of the arrow-pierced mercenary with a lateral swipe of the sword, the shimmering blue blade cutting him neatly in half. Hearing the multiple thrum of crossbow strings, Guyime spun, the sword's glow adding to the general confusion as it cut a half-dozen bolts from the air. He launched himself at the nearest mercenary who had unwisely opted to try and reload his crossbow rather than reach for his sword, not that it would have availed him much in any case.

Lopping off the upper portion of his skull, Guyime ducked under a well-executed halberd thrust delivered by one of his comrades and replied with an upward sweep of the sword, bisecting both the stave of the weapon and the man who held it. He charged on, following a downward spiral towards the heart, the sword moving of its own volition to deflect another salvo of crossbow bolts before wreaking havoc on their owners. When a dozen or more mercenaries lay dead, it was sufficient evidence to the survivors that continuing with this particular contract was not worth the reward in comparison to the risk. Within seconds they had fled, some casting their weapons away in their haste.

What a feast you bring me, my liege, Lakorath commented in sated appreciation as the blood slicking the blade sublimed into the steel. *Some acrid notes, but it all adds to the complexity of the flavour.*

"Get away from her!"

The tearful, enraged shout drew his gaze towards the heart, now beating at such a tempo that its glow was near constant. Calandra's slumped, unmoving form lay before it, one hand clutching the sword to her chest, her struggles with the demon it contained apparently over. Lexius stood between her and the advancing silhouette of her father. In the heart's glow, the slave's thick lenses rendered his eyes into twin discs of fire, his teeth bared in a feral snarl.

"Stand aside," his master ordered in curt dismissal, striding towards his daughter with unhesitant authority. Guyime saw him draw a dagger from the folds of his robe as he uttered a final word, "Slave."

Seeing Seeker raise her bow to draw a bead on the queyo, Guyime raised a hand. "Wait!"

Eager for more entertainment, my liege? Lakorath enquired as the two figures closed.

"He should have the chance to break his own chains," Guyime replied, watching the ugly and untidy struggle unfold.

Vatori at first tried to slash his way past Lexius, swiping at his neck with deft strokes of his dagger. Lexius, however, no longer had any use for such subtlety. Guyime saw him suffer a flurry of cuts to his face and arms as he launched himself at his master, claws hands lashing at Vatori's eyes, his attack accompanied by an animalistic snarl. The queyo's face became a mask of rage and disgust as he reeled back from the assault, blood appearing on his brow and cheek before he managed to catch hold of Lexius's wrist, delivering a hard kick to the slave's gut in the same instant. Before he could raise the dagger for a killing blow, Lexius craned his neck to latch his teeth onto the hand that held the weapon, biting deep, jaws worrying like a bulldog with a captive rabbit.

Metal chimed on stone as the dagger fell from Vatori's maimed hand, the sound swallowed by the high-pitched scream erupting from his throat, now rich in fear rather than anger. He tried to pull away but Lexius moved with savage agility, springing up to wrap his arms and legs around his master's torso. Guyime caught sight of the slave's features as he reared, the blood that covered them black in the heart's glow, teeth gleaming and jaw gaping wide.

Vatori's scream became a gurgle as Lexius's teeth found his throat, gnawing through skin, tendon and vein in a frenzy. Guyime knew his ferocity owed much to his early life and the contest that had placed him in Vatori's clutches, but owed more to the woman who lay senseless and probably dead a few feet away.

Lexius continued to rend at Vatori's neck as the queyo collapsed, features slack and eyes empty. He left off at the sound of Guyime's footfalls, sitting back on the corpse, chest heaving and face raised. Guyime saw no triumph on his gore-covered features, no exultation at his new-won freedom. His ferocity vanished as quickly as it dawned, leaving behind a man with much to grieve over.

They stared at each other for a time in wordless and mutual understanding until Lexius's gaze slipped to the dead man beneath him, a small twitch of shame passing over his bloodied face. "She could never hate him," he said, voice hoarse. "Despite all I revealed about his plans, all he had ordained for her and our plotting against him, she still couldn't hate him. I don't think it was in her." He wiped a mingling of flesh and blood from his lips and stared at his filth-covered hands. "But it seems I had enough for both of us."

"She's still breathing."

Seeker crouched at Calandra's side, holding a hand to her forehead. "It's faint," she added as Lexius and Guyime hurried to join her. She met Guyime's questioning frown and gave a slight shake of her head. Like him, she had well-honed instincts when it came to the imminence of death.

"Calandra..." Lexius reached out a tentative hand to cup the mage's bleached face. Her eyelids fluttered open in response, lips parting to emit a very small sigh. "It's gone..." she whispered, her hand grasping feebly at the hilt of the sword resting on her chest. "Only way...to drive it out..." Her lips curved a little before her face tensed and she jerked with a final upsurge of strength, gripping his hand and forcing the sword into it.

Lexius stiffened at the touch of the sword's handle, his slight frame convulsing in a manner Guyime knew all too well; bonding a human soul to a magical artefact was ever a painful business.

Calandra and Lexius stared into each other's unblinking eyes, the sword held between them until the light faded from her gaze and she slumped into death.

Lexius shuddered again as her hands slipped from the sword, sagging in sorrow but then abruptly taking on a statue-like stillness as the stahlius blade gave off a small flicker. It was different in hue to Guyime's blade, both lighter and somehow more vibrant. Lexius let out a gasp as the tremulous glow built into a steady, unwavering luminescence.

"I... I know," he said, and Guyime knew he spoke in answer to a question only he could hear. The blade he held might still be termed cursed, but it was no longer inhabited by a demon.

Lexius nodded in answer to yet more unheard words, his gaze shifting to the heart which was now glowing brighter than ever, the air around it starting to shimmer with released energy. "She says he'll be fully awake soon," the former slave said, getting to his feet. "He's very angry."

He lowered his eyes to the body of the woman who he had called mistress, the woman who had loved him enough to die for his freedom. "She says we should go," Lexius grated through clenched teeth as he forced himself to turn away.

Chapter 11

CARTHULA'S FALL

◦)━━━(◦)━━━(◦

At Lexius's urging they ran up the slope, clearing the stone bowl only seconds before the heart exploded. The unleashed power formed an expanding circle of roiling crimson energy that shattered all but the stoutest rock. Boulders the size of houses plummeted from the cavern ceiling, Guyime glancing up to see sunlight slanting through the expanding gaps. Several times the ground beneath their feet shook with enough violence to send them tumbling.

A hazardous sprint finally brought them to the cavern where the remnants of the maze waited just in time to watch the entire jagged expanse collapse into the void. The thunderous din of its demise was soon overwhelmed by the roar of rushing water as the sea invaded the sundered bowels of Carthula. Staggering to the edge of the newly formed cliff, Guyime gazed down at a heaving swell, roiling with the continuing rain of debris from above. He could see more than just rocks amongst the dark cascade now; household sundries plummeted amongst the stunned or screaming bodies of their owners. Not all were fortunate to simply plunge into an uncertain fate amongst the waves. Guyime winced at the sight of dozens colliding with the many columns of granite that had survived the final cataclysmic pulse of the kraken's heart.

Turning about, he saw that they were now marooned on a small plateau. The bowl and the cavern that housed it had vanished into the sea, bathed in light from revealed sky that streamed through what had been the centre of Carthula. The waters that had flooded the bowl had formed a great swirl, the waves coiling and spinning with a speed and force he knew could never be natural. The suspicion was confirmed when the waves turned to vapour as something vast erupted through the surface with a roar that banished all other noise.

Steam blossomed as the mighty shape heaved itself from the waves, formed of shifting clouds of red energy that boiled and scorched everything they touched. It was too insubstantial to make out clear details, but Guyime discerned a pair of furious glowing eyes and a gaping maw of many teeth before the whole spectacle surged up into what remained of the city above.

Whilst much of the city's central islet had collapsed, many neighbourhoods near the fringes survived, Guyime making out hordes of panicked people clustered on balconies or rooftops. The roar of the kraken's ghost as it swept from the waves to claim its vengeance swallowed their screams, but Guyime felt he heard them nonetheless. Houses burned and shattered and people fell like embers as the beast thrashed its way from one cluster of buildings to another. It appeared to shrink as it slaughtered and destroyed, as if its lust for retribution leeched away with every life it took.

When the final cascade of corpses and rubble had fallen into the sea, Guyime saw the red, steaming spectre, now reduced to merely elephantine proportions, pause for a second to survey its handiwork. The glowing red eyes swept over the smoking remains of Carthula's heart, either in satisfaction or regret Guyime couldn't tell. Then, with a final roar, it dove from its perch amidst the piled rubble, streaking down through the gaping chasm where the city's wealthiest had lived to birth a towering column of steam as it plunged into the sea.

"He was very angry," Lexius repeated. He sat slumped near the edge of the plateau, the Kraken's Tooth cradled in his arms in a manner that told Guyime he would never be parted from it, not that such a thing was possible now.

Poor bastard, Lakorath commented. *Shackled to the same mate forever. Surely the greatest ever test of true love, eh, my liege?*

"Not forever," Guyime said. "Just until we find the other swords."

You're still intent upon that? The sword gave a resentful shudder as Guyime returned him to the sheath on his back. *After all this.*

"This course is set and we are bound to it," Guyime reminded him, reaching into his jacket for the Cartographer's map, unfurling it to gauge their next course. He glanced up at the sound of Seeker's voice.

"My daughter," she said to Lexius. "I'm told you know where she is."

Lexius blinked at her, his features resuming their old inexpressive self as he replied, "Purchased by one Ultrius Carvaro, a noted merchant and patron of the arts resident in…"

"Atheria," Guyime interrupted, holding up the chart, its swirling lines tracking northeast from Carthula to the port known as the City of Songs.

"Yes." Lexius got to his feet, squinting hard at the chart. Grief, apparently, couldn't stem his curiosity. "What is that?"

"The map of our shared purpose," Guyime told him. "If you're willing. As a free man you can do as you wish."

"Shared purpose?"

"The Seven Swords…" Guyime began.

"That'll have to wait," Seeker cut in, nodding to the sea below their refuge where a fishing smack was ploughing its way through the choppy swell. The man standing on the boat's prow raised a hand in greeting. As the boat neared the craggy shore of this freshly made cliff, the wind filling its sails abruptly died, reducing its progress to a gentle bob.

"Nice day for a little seaborne excursion, wouldn't y'say?" Lorweth called up to them. "The captain of this fine vessel was kind enough to grant me passage, provided I fill his sails all the way to harbours new. Seems he doesn't see much of a future in these waters."

He let out a hearty laugh which Guyime failed to return. "What do you want, druid?"

"Why, to offer a safe berth and passage, o'course." Lorweth twirled his hand and bent his back in a florid bow. "Assuming you've got something to trade for it. Y'did claim the sword, I take it?"

"No." Guyime nodded to Lexius. "He did. And it's not for sale."

"Pity." Lorweth's gaze tracked over the three of them, frowning. "The lovely mage-ess didn't survive her father's scheme then? A shame, and not a thing I'm proud of, just so y'know. Still," he bowed again, not so ostentatiously, and turned away, "I've always been a man who expects payment in all things…"

Lexius pointed the stahlius at the sea off the boat's port bow, lightning crackling along the blade then erupting from the triangular point in a concentrated stream that birthed a tall spout of water when it met the sea.

"My wife appreciates your regrets," Lexius called down to Lorweth. "And asks how you intend to sail to ports new without a boat."

"Right then," Lorweth said, briskly clapping his hands together. "Best get y'selves aboard and we'll be off."

Seeker slung her bow across her back before launching herself over the cliff in a flawless dive. Watching her swim to the boat and climb aboard. Guyime felt little surprise at the sight of a feline form slinking from a shadowed corner of the deck to jump into her arms. Lissah, as predicted, would always find a way.

"The Seven Swords represent a complex web of history and fable," Lexius said as Guyime prepared to jump. "Some of it I know to be true, much of the rest hard to credit."

"Then come with me and sort truth from fable."

"And if you succeed in finding them all, what then?" Lexius inclined his head at the ruin of Carthula. The central islet had disappeared but for a dozen sea stacks that seemed so fragile they might tumble into the sea at any second. The outer ring of linked islets was mostly intact, however, their clifftops and balconies crowded with people standing in silent vigil of their vanished betters. "Finding just one of the seven wrought all of this," Lexius observed. "Not a promising omen."

"A good many people died and that's a tragedy," Guyime said. "But who were they? Greedy merchant houses locked in a never-ending and deadly game for dominance. And how many slave chains were broken today? As for the swords' purpose." He shook his head. "I don't know yet. But I know it calls to me, and her," he nodded to Seeker on the boat, "and now you, and the soul of the woman you love."

Lexius looked at the sword in his hand, the blade shimmering in response, its glow less bright than before. "She says she can hear some of your demon's thoughts," Lexius reported. "She doesn't like it."

"Then she has very good judgment."

Guyime stepped to the cliff edge, turning to extend his hand. "When last I visited the City of Songs, I listened to bards recite odes celebrating the virtues of liberty within earshot of the largest slave market in all of the Third Sea. That's a great many chains to break for a man with a mage-blessed sword."

"As long as you find another sword in the process?"

"Yes." Guyime continued to hold out his hand, watching Lexius cast a final glance at the city that had been his home and his prison, now forever changed. Sighing, he looked away, glancing briefly at Guyime's hand.

"I can't swim," he said, raising the sword. Lightning flashed over the blade once more and Lexius flew, arcing over the surf to land untidily on the deck of the boat, drawing a loud laugh from Lorweth in the process.

Chains to break, my liege? Lakorath asked as Guyime launched himself from the cliff edge. *Has this obsession become a crusade now? They rarely bring out the best in you, as I recall.*

The icy chill of the sea was bracing and the weight of the sword on his back a fierce burden, dragging him deep before he clawed his way back to the surface. But it was a burden he had long endured and would for however long his purpose required.

"No," he agreed, spitting salted water from his mouth as he broke through the waves and struck out towards the boat. "But, to find the swords, I've a sense I'll need to be at my worst before this is over."